Gritty, funny, sad and uplifting. A great story about food, family and finding your way.

—**KEVIN SYLVESTER,** bestselling author
of the *MiNRS Trilogy*

Wayne Ng delivers in giving us an authentic glimpse into the struggles and racism faced by Chinese immigrants in Toronto in 1977 through the eyes of a spirited teenager whom you will root for.

—**JENNILEE AUSTRIA-BONIFACIO,** CBC Reads
longlisted for *Reuniting with Strangers*

In a much awaited sequel to his award-winning novel *Letters from Johnny,* Wayne Ng introduces us to an older Johnny balancing family debt and the drug under-world. The complexity of Asian family dynamics are revealed through concise dialogues. Much is left unsaid. Family secrets are tenaciously guarded or simply brushed off. Humour is used as a defence mechanism. As a Vietnamese-Canadian, I understand well this wall of silence permeating first generation immigrants. Ng writes with authenticity. He writes from the heart. To under-stand Johnny's dilemma is to understand the immigrant experience. *Johnny Delivers* should be on all reading lists.

—**CAROLINE VU,** Hugh McLennan Prize finalist
for *Catinat Boulevard*

Family secrets, cultural identity, racism, and crime collide in this coming of age story that is equal parts funny and vexing. I was charmed by Johnny's compassion and good intentions, and I read with increasing anxiety as his ambition causes the walls to close in. A fascinating portrayal of an immigrant family's experience of Toronto in the 70s, *Johnny Delivers* is thought-provoking, heartfelt, and highly entertaining.

—**KATE A BOORMAN,** award-winning author
of *Winterkill*

Essential Prose Series 220

Canada Council **Conseil des Arts**
for the Arts **du Canada**

ONTARIO ARTS COUNCIL
CONSEIL DES ARTS DE L'ONTARIO

an Ontario government agency
un organisme du gouvernement de l'Ontario

Canadä

Guernica Editions Inc. acknowledges the support of the Canada Council
for the Arts and the Ontario Arts Council. The Ontario Arts Council
is an agency of the Government of Ontario.

We acknowledge the financial support of the Government of Canada.

Johnny Delivers

WAYNE NG

GUERNICA
EDITIONS
TORONTO · CHICAGO · BUFFALO · LANCASTER (U.K.)
2024

Guernica Founder: Antonio D'Alfonso

Michael Mirolla, general editor
Margo LaPierre, editor
David Moratto, interior and cover design

Guernica Editions Inc.
1241 Marble Rock Rd., Gananoque, ON K7G 2V4
2250 Military Road, Tonawanda, N.Y. 14150-6000 U.S.A.
www.guernicaeditions.com

Distributors:
Independent Publishers Group (IPG)
600 North Pulaski Road, Chicago IL 60624
University of Toronto Press Distribution (UTP)
5201 Dufferin Street, Toronto (ON), Canada M3H 5T8

First edition.
Printed in Canada.

Legal Deposit—Third Quarter
Library of Congress Catalog Card Number: 2024933681
Library and Archives Canada Cataloguing in Publication
Title: Johnny delivers / Wayne Ng.
Names: Ng, Wayne, author.
Series: Essential prose series ; 220.
Description: Series statement: Essential prose series ; 220
Identifiers: Canadiana (print) 20240332180 |
Canadiana (ebook) 20240332210 | ISBN 9781771838900 (softcover) |
ISBN 9781771838917 (EPUB)
Subjects: LCGFT: Novels.
Classification: LCC PS8627.G318 J64 2024 | DDC C813/.6—dc23

*For all the paper families
and their untold stories.*

Chapter 1

Firstborn Bummer

"JOHNNY, GO FIND your mama," Baba said, a cigarette dangling from his lower lip as he flipped over several orders of eggs.

"What?" I lowered the volume on the radio, which had been counting down the Top 40. The Emotions got knocked off number one by Andy Gibb. Unbelievable.

Baba's pissy tone meant Mama wasn't working breakfast. She likely stayed out last night. It used to be that, when either Baba or I were crabby or stressed, we'd try to chill each other out by playfully jousting with Bruce Lee proverbs.

"Be like water," he'd say to me.

"Not until you empty your mind, Baba."

"If you spend too much time thinking about it, you'll never get it done, son."

We'd grab a cup and say, "Like this cup, you are full of opinions." Then we'd look at Mama and whisper, "Most people can talk without listening. Very few can listen without talking." We'd crack up and snicker at her.

We replaced that with silence years ago.

Mama's always taken off. I remember when I was young, and Baba had been gone for years already, she'd wait for me to fall asleep, then sneak out to play mahjong. She would return smelling like Johnnie Walker if she'd lost, or carrying wonton soup and humming opera if she'd won.

She stopped drinking once Baba suddenly returned home with a huge surprise, and I don't mean a good one. I was eleven. Try coming home from school and finding out you have a younger sister named Jane, who's messing around with your toys. I'm not kidding.

I don't care much when Mama sneaks off, even though I'm left to work the grill or the cash in her place. School's boring as hell, and the restaurant is my future.

I asked Baba, "Why can't *Jane* find Mama? Why can't *Jane* work more?"

"Jane is too busy. She has piano and lots of homework. She is an A+ student and can't fall below. Besides, you are a much better worker."

I'm glad he spared me another big speech about the duties and responsibilities of being the eldest and a male. In Canadian Family Studies, the teacher said firstborns could look forward to making more money and going further in school than their siblings. Really? I guess those firstborns figured out how to weasel out of taking the wheel at their sad-sack family businesses. And when they weaseled out, their ancestors weren't rolling over in their graves. Do you know why I know this? Because the teacher wasn't talking about Chinese families!

And to rub it all in, there's Jane's goody-two-shoes routine. I have to give it to her, she plays it well. Being second-born means you can do sweet dick all and still win. She once almost burned down the neighbourhood. Even then, Baba made it seem like nothing happened. As long as I've known him, she's been duping him with her "perfect daughter, perfect student" schtick. Mama's too sharp to fall for that, so it's Baba who deals with Daddy's girl.

"You handle your mama the best," Baba said to me. "See this?" He pointed to his balding head. "I am the first Wong to lose his hair. All our ancestors had hair. Even your wild great-uncle had hair. Your mama did this to me. Only you can find her."

Chapter 2

Leo

I'M ALWAYS EITHER refereeing my parents or looking out for them. Like when Mama takes off after we all go to bed. I used to check for her floral slippers by the door when I'd wake up at night. If they weren't there, that meant she'd snuck in, home safe, and had gone to bed. Twice, Baba caught me up waiting for her. I let him think I was sleepwalking and did some of Bruce's rapid air punches. Of course, Bruce was punching alongside me, adjusting my hips and raising my elbows, ready to smack me if I took my eyes off the opponent.

Over time, I got used to not knowing where Mama was. I got better at sleeping. And yet, each morning, I still check for her slippers.

Mama has lots of hangout spots, like the back of King's Noodle, which usually has some games going on and serves scotch in chipped teacups after-hours. There's also Ying Ying Soy, whose owner was on the same boat as Mama when she came over. But this time, I figured she could be found at the bottom of Huron Street, a few blocks south of Chinatown's main drag on Dundas.

She's there so often it's like she'd rather be there than with us. I parked our shitbox delivery car, the Vega, in front of a string of row houses and noticed a new steel door with freshly painted characters: Wong Association.

Auntie works in one of the smaller and newer associations. She's not my for-real aunt. Although, somewhere, way back, most Wongs are blood. My uncle and a bunch of elders figured they'd never make it to the executive of the really big Wong Association, so years ago, they splintered off. That was a big deal, like walking away from your family. They took over the old row house from an aging bachelor who used to use it as a rooming house. They converted it into a small community hub for Wongs, who were more interested in gambling and dishing out high-interest loans than housing tenants. Unlike the other associations, Auntie has started to run some big games, drawing people in from other associations and off the street.

At first, she'd kept the games small and quiet so the police wouldn't raid them. The recently arrived triad gangs couldn't be bothered with extorting such small fish. But higher-stakes games happen at her association all the time now, so you'd think they'd draw attention sooner or later.

But you'd probably also think her place was just another run-down house with a saggy porch and peeling shingles. This one had Leo guarding the door. I stepped up and said hello. He had a collection of bowling shirts with different name tags pinned on. Today, Leo was Joe. He was leaning against the wall, reading a *Fantastic Four* comic. Beside him, also leaning against the wall, was a rusty steel pipe—that was new.

He lit a smoke and offered me one. I waved it off. Leo and I were once two of the few CBCs (Canadian-born Chinese) at Central Tech, even though, in 1977, it was the biggest high school in Canada. The FOBs (fresh-off-the-boaters) from Hong Kong always made us CBCs look nerdy. Leo and I started to connect more when I was a niner. We found each other sitting outside the vice principal's office. He was there for fighting, me for talking back to Mr. Cameron again. Leo didn't care about anything, and I couldn't keep my mouth shut or stay focused for long. Trevor Heywood had just come out of the VP's office. He laughed at us and said he couldn't tell us apart. I didn't stop to think that he was a lineman on the bantam football team—I just got up and smacked him. Trevor shoved me hard against the wall, banging my head. It was worth it, though, because Leo and I have been cool ever since.

What's unusual about Leo is that he's an only child. That's rare in Chinese families. Come to think of it, if not for Jane, who's only a half sister, I'd be an only child, too. A streetcar killed Leo's dad. It happened right before Mama started hanging around the Association more.

At first, I thought Leo was a social reject, like Boo Radley in *To Kill a Mockingbird* or that dense but well-intentioned Charlie Gordon in *Flowers for Algernon*. But he's way smarter than he lets on. He dropped out of school after his father died. He'd never been able to hold a job until his mother made him work the door at the Association. At least Leo had found something steady that wasn't bagging submarine buns at Silverstein's for $2.30 an hour.

I asked him if Mama was there.

"Yeah, still. She hung around all night, played most of the night. I think she broke even. It's bitchin' seeing her play for the high-scoring combos."

"Go big or go home. That's my mother, the legend." Mama is supposedly the only person to have ever assembled a jee moh—a thirteen orphans hand. It's the ultimate badass hand, relying on self-drawing every tile, including the winning fourteenth tile. It means everyone loses to you and has to pay, so you triple your winnings. A jee moh shows extreme patience, self-reliance, and luck. She always said you have to be good to be lucky. She has neither denied nor confirmed she ever pulled that hand off, so it's like everything else about her—a mystery.

Mama has tried to teach me her "go big or go home" style of play during our family mahjong nights. Auntie has warned me Mama's style is reckless and has tried to school me in a more strategic, calculating game. Now I understand the benefits of both.

Leo asked me, "Did you know she's way behind on her loan?"

"What loan?"

"The five grand she took out six months ago. Your restaurant was put up as collateral. You mean you didn't know?"

I held my breath for a second. "You faking me out?"

"It's not a joke. Loans have to be paid back—on time." Leo ground his cigarette with his kung fu shoe. "The elders are going to want this cleared up. They may send my mama to talk to your dad."

"Don't," I pleaded. I hadn't known about the loan, so sure as heck, Baba doesn't either. He'd freak. That would lead to an epic fight. Baba hated two things more than anything: 1) cheap customers who lingered and 2) owing money, especially to the Association.

Baba walked out when I was a little boy. After he returned a million years later with Jane, I was never sure he would stay. When Jane turned out to be a seven-year-old pyromaniac, I thought Mama would kick them out or take off herself. Every fight since, I've checked to see if the suitcases were gone. Either one of them could snap and run.

"Come on, Leo, we're family. She'll pay the house back."

He scratched at his uneven moustache. "Your mama always comes with a smile and a treat, like I'm gold. If it were up to me, no problem, I'd look the other way. My mother can't keep covering for her. It's not personal. It's business."

Mama gave Leo the gold-plated treatment every time she saw him. I mean, once in a while—yes. An aunt is supposed to do that. But what about me? I'm her kid.

We exchanged nods. As much as I hated the message, I still felt like there was something good between us, something core and old.

But I didn't have five thousand dollars lying around, and judging by the look in Leo's squint, he knew it.

"No family discount anymore, Johnny."

I didn't like how his tone had shifted. "What does that mean?"

"It means you guys are in a pile of deep shit."

Damn. "I got this, Leo, just give me some time."

He chuckled. "Who do you think you are, Radar?"

That guy in *M*A*S*H* who's always a step ahead of everybody. Leo had a point. That wasn't me.

"I doubt you got a box full of stuffed lai see under your bed," he said. "Trust me, you won't be the one to make this all go away."

Mama had put the restaurant on the line. What trouble had she gotten us into?

Chapter 3

The Association

LEO LED ME inside the converted row house. He told me Mama was sleeping like a baby in the upstairs break room, so I wasn't especially worried. I had to walk around one of the homeless men squatting on the floor. He probably came to score a free bowl of congee and to check the job-and-message board. For many members, the board was the only way to send and receive mail from home, a buddy, the government, or whatever.

As usual, the stench of Tiger Balm, the mustiness of a Salvation Army store, and cigarette smoke hung together. If old age doesn't kill the uncles, the air quality will.

I used to wonder why they didn't stay home and watch TV. Then I learned that most of the uncles don't even have a TV. They only have each other. The tongs, or associations, are supposed to be like traditional Chinese clubs—running on donations and volunteers. Every member coughs up a small annual due. Mama used to help in one of them, sewing, cooking, and stuff. The clubs provide a safe place to hang out or if a member gets kicked out of the house and needs a place to crash.

Chinatowns and tongs began after the railroad was done. The Chinese labourers were still getting crapped on by the gwai lo. So the uncles clustered together, forming their neighbourhoods. Then, the Canadian government stopped Chinese immigration, permanently separating the remaining Chinese, mostly older men, from their families in China. Pretty sad.

I know a thing or two about a family being separated. Enough to say this: the uncles swallowed their emptiness like rancid meat they couldn't vomit. They banded together and formed support groups based on clans to keep each other going through those long, difficult years when they were segregated and couldn't vote, hold office, or own property—a whole bunch of unfair stuff. Nobody likes to talk about it now, as if doing so might conjure up evil demons.

Red scrolls with black calligraphy adorn the faded jade-green walls, probably some Confucius saying. The writing could be an egg-salad recipe for all I know. I can't read much Chinese. Mama gave me the choice to spend my Saturday mornings learning the tens of thousands of characters in school or watching cartoons. Guess what I picked? *Scooby-Dooby Doooo!*

Pictures of stern-faced elders and the Association's executive lined another wall. Opposite that was a table with a bouquet of joss sticks planted in a ceramic urn and a huge painting of the five fierce muscled-up generals staring down at us mortals. They used to be ordinary, but after destroying the bad guys, they achieved super-level righteousness and Godlike status. Every Chinese home hangs a calendar of them. Those badasses would've been hard for Bruce Lee to take down, but he'd have found a way.

"Ah baak." I waved at Uncle Kwong and several of the other uncles, who waved back. Uncle Kwong had a massive bald head and age spots all over his face like barnacles. He hadn't helped build the railroad, but he sure looked like he had. He and the other uncles spent the entire day reading old newspapers, gossiping, and playing mahjong together. They'll do the same thing tomorrow, the day after that, and the day after that. They've had the same routine for years. Someday, that might be me.

Jane told me once she thought they were creepy, that she hates how they paw at us like we're zoo creatures. It's not like the uncles are perverts or anything. They're just old, and they miss their family back in China.

Baba said old-timers like Uncle Kwong got into Canada before the Exclusion Act shut the door to all Chinese. After the war ended, the Chinese could enter Canada again, but they had to be the family of Canadian citizens. Many Chinese bought false documents claiming to be the sons or daughters of citizens. When Baba came as a kid, he was a paper son, but he won't talk about it. For many of them, once they got here, they were all alone. It was the associations that stepped in to help them launch their lives.

Jane's wrong about the uncles. I know better. They see us as rare museum pieces to be treasured. They spoil us with sweet treats like White Rabbit or Haw Flakes. They remind us to listen to our parents, study hard, and stay out of trouble. Uncle Kwong slips me the odd quarter for being good. A quarter was like a million dollars to me for a long time, and probably still is to him.

Baba said that, after decades here with nothing to show for it but their broken bodies, most of them couldn't go home and face their families. So they grew old together, like married bachelors who'd left their children behind, an ocean and a continent away. Still, time and distance couldn't corrode their loyalty to family. It's pretty sad, though, like I said, knowing guys like Uncle Kwong who did nothing but keep their heads down while other people called the shots.

It's been a long time since I got a quarter. But occasionally, Uncle Kwong tears up and reaches out for a hug. Like Jane, that used to freak me out when I was little. But I let him hug me because I like the idea of making him happy, and he rewards me with a toothless smile.

The serious games take place upstairs in small rooms, their windows covered with Chinese dailies. Auntie likes having me around and always lets me go up to watch Mama play.

I went straight to the lounge, where players take breaks. Mama was sleeping like a baby on a cot. Let her sleep, I figured. I went in to see the real action—the mahjong games.

Chapter 4

The Games

I HADN'T WATCHED a game in a while, but I recognized the players: Auntie, of course; Mr. Ho, who started coming regularly a few months ago; Mr. Lam; and the herbalist from down the street.

Mr. Ho and Mr. Lam were chatting about a horse race, at least that's what it sounded like. Mr. Ho's Hong Kong Cantonese is educated and refined compared to our Toisanese village dialect. It's like comparing a Toronto-born city slicker to an Albertan raised by wolves. At least they weren't speaking Mandarin, which would've been Greek to me.

Lately, more and more Hong Kongers have been coming over. Mama thinks they're a bunch of snooty show-offs who don't respect the road that the Toisanese paved and have been toiling over starting a hundred years ago. It shocked the hell out of me that she knew anything about Chinese history in Canada. She said she learned it from a customer. As for me, I know sweet dick all.

Auntie had her back to the far wall, a cigarette hanging on for dear life out the corner of her mouth. A visor shielded her eyes, though you always feel her watching you.

I studied the table. Students at a chemistry lecture show more emotion than serious mahjongers.

I could see Auntie's play. She wanted a high-scoring hand. It was obvious to me, but the others played like amateurs. I knew I could take Auntie if I ever had the money or the balls.

"Pung!" Mr. Ho shouted as he picked up a discard to complete a three of a kind. He scanned the exposed tiles on the table, calculating the probabilities behind his next move. His body shifted, probably anticipating victory, as he tossed down a last, extraneous Red Dragon— the fool.

Auntie smirked. "Sik wu."

Auntie had been playing a concealed hand, revealing nothing. Most players have their tiles facing them and in some order, like in gin rummy. Every once in a while, when the stakes are high, Auntie will keep her tiles down and not even look at them. You can watch her thumb feeling the engravings, but she won't even bother to line them up in any order. Instead of organizing them into possible sets like everybody else, she'll repeatedly shift her tiles. That kind of trick doesn't scare me, but it's an effective psych against some.

Auntie had stolen Mr. Ho's win. He grudgingly pushed some tens and twenties across the table her way.

The tiles were moved back into the centre of the table and shuffled for the next round. Auntie got up and stretched before smiling and waving me over.

She has this thing about being in people's faces, like inches away. You can't really back away to avoid her signature smell of green onions and cigarettes. Mama says it's to intimidate people, but I've never felt that way. Auntie can be crusty on the outside, but she's always been decent to me. Plus, she makes me feel like a son. I'm sure that pisses Mama off. Maybe that's part of their cold war.

Chapter 5

One Bad Streak

"Ah yi, how are you?" I said in my best Toisanese as I half bowed my head.

"Such a good boy." Auntie took a drag of her cigarette before exhaling.

Such praise was code for *don't embarrass the family, listen to your parents and look after them*, even if it meant doing something you didn't want to do.

"Thank you, ah yi."

She handed me a cup of tea, and we chatted about school. She kidded about all the girls chasing me. I wished.

"My Leo talk to you?" she asked.

"Yes, ah yi, I'll look after this, thank you."

"Very good. I'm worried about your mama." She sighed. "The uncles are pressuring me to collect. I can only protect her for so long. We have been patient."

"What do you mean?"

She switched to English and whispered, "This is not a bank. This is not a charity."

The Association *was* a bit of a charity. Every member floated a few dollars a month into a pool for whoever needed a loan. If you didn't repay the loan, you were shorting members, friends, and the community. Social ostracization and a loss of face were enough to keep things moving.

Then, a recent bombing at a Chinese restaurant on Elizabeth Street killed one guy and injured three others. That kind of stuff never happened before the triads arrived, so everyone assumed it was them moving into moneylending. I read in the *Toronto Star* how those gangsters controlled Hong Kong and so many Chinatowns in North America. It makes me wonder if the newspapers are dreaming up another Yellow Peril scare or if what they've been reporting is really happening.

"What are you saying, Auntie?"

She sighed. "Be careful. The uncles are cracking down on derelict debts. What if they choose to make an example of your family?"

Leo had said the restaurant was the collateral. That meant that, if Baba and Mama defaulted, the Association could, in a roundabout way, wind up with the restaurant. It stunned me that the uncles would suddenly play hardball like that. I thanked Auntie for her concern.

"I hear the Red Pagoda now delivers," she said. "Offers combo-nation plates. Business must be good."

"Yes, prosperity is just around the corner." The bullshit fortune cookie stuff that comes out of our mouths blows me away sometimes.

"We all want prosperity. When your mother first came to us from the village, she was very naïve, painfully shy, curious, and ambitious. I tried to protect her then, too. But curiosity and ambition can lead a person astray. Why must all teenagers be so rash? I'm just glad my Johnny is different." She pinched my cheek, leading me to roll my head abashedly. "I've said too much. Why rehash the past, right?" She swatted at the air as though chasing away a sour memory.

Astray? It was nice that Auntie trusted me enough to even say that. Mama would freak out if she knew Auntie had said that about her. It was a bit weird she'd talk about my mama to me like that, but I'd rather have things out in the open than mysteriously shoved under the rug. Like Leo's dad—he's an ancestor now, but nobody in my family ever speaks about him. It was after he died that Mama joined the ladies' group and started going to the Association regularly.

Auntie switched back to Toisanese. "If you and your mama cannot figure out this debt very soon, they may send me to visit your baba." She paused and let that sink in. "Please, Johnny, you and your mama are important to me. Do not let it come to this."

"Yes, ah yi."

"One bad streak, and that little restaurant could land in someone else's hands." She shook her head.

Losing the restaurant would crush Baba. He and Mama would blame each other and break up again. That would be awful. I had to do something.

"But I could help you, Johnny." Auntie's face lit up like a schoolgirl who'd been picked first. "We could find a place for you here. Come work for me instead."

An unexpected shiver ran up my spine. I forced a smile and a half bow. "I could not possibly deserve such a position. My place is with my family."

I proceeded to back away, and then Auntie slipped a ten-spot into my hand.

"Don't say anything to Leo." She winked.

She could always be counted on for a little bit of extra cash.

Mama, in the empty room, struggled to wake up at first. But she shot right up when Auntie tried to help by nudging and calling her. She batted Auntie's hand away like it was radioactive. There were times I wished they'd cat-fight and be done with it. I helped Mama into the car. She looked back like she'd forgotten something, but the sight of Leo casually leaning against the door snapped her out of whatever headspace she was in.

Chapter 6

No Getting Soft

MAYBE BRUCE LEE will know what to do. Yeah, I know he's been dead four years. He died on July 20, 1973. They say it was brain swelling. It was a Saturday morning when Baba, terrified, charged into my room with the news. A day that will live in infamy for all Chinese. Imagine Kennedy and Elvis dying together in a car accident. The gwai lo world would be crying for weeks. That would be almost as big.

He may be dead, but he comes around once in a while, usually when I get bummed out, which happens more often lately. He looks great, sounds great, has quite the temper, and is cocky as shit. But then again, he's Bruce Lee.

I'm not weird. At least, I hope not. Bruce said I should think less and show more "emotional content." So, I got cheeky and excitedly told him the Leafs would win the Cup. He smiled and threatened to kick my butt. I wasn't worried. He's only in my head. Nobody else can see or hear him. Once in a while I forget people can hear me talking out loud to him. Sometimes, he's like a devil on my shoulder, telling me to skip class and go out for a smoke like he's one of us in grade twelve. Other times, he's a Shaolin monk on the other shoulder, dispensing wisdom.

I wonder if Hollywood would have given him his due if he had lived. Had his mysterious, premature death made him even bigger than he might've been? Either way, if he were still alive, things would be different between me and Baba.

"I would've been the number-one star in the world," Bruce said, sweating in his white undershirt. He took out his nunchucks and did one of his routines—taking out a group of thugs like he did in *The Way of the Dragon*.

"I was bigger than the Beatles in Asia. I would've been on *Johnny Carson*. There would've been a cartoon series and action figures. A new Barbie line would've come out, featuring me kicking Ken's butt and marrying Barbie. Don't tell Linda." He winked as he finished off with a heel kick and one of his patented cat shrieks. A beautiful blonde fell into his outstretched arm.

Like I said, cocky as shit.

Against bad guys and the ladies, Bruce had all the right moves. The only moves I know are the robot and the camel walk. And I can only do them when I'm alone in my bedroom.

Bruce isn't just a movie star. He also wrote one of my favourite books, *Tao of Jeet Kune Do*. It's about the principles and philosophy behind martial arts, and tapping into what you're good at. He inspired me to start working out. He also showed me that it was cool to write. So, I started that too. Mostly essays for the school rag. Writing helps me get things off my chest, like my issues with my family, which is falling apart, as usual. It'll be on me to bail them out again. That's the Kato role I must play, cleaning up after other people.

Most of us are playing roles and don't realize it. For the Chinese, it might be running a restaurant or something involving math. Bonus points if you can combine both. We play along with the stereotype, remaining humble without drawing any attention or hassle. To do otherwise brings grief to the community. No group rehearsals are necessary. The parts are safe and for life, so long as we stick to our lines. It all seems natural, like it's in our DNA. Occasionally, a mutant strand appears. A Chinese lawyer or a politician. Then you wonder if they had a white mom or dad or were born rich.

I guess Bruce was a full-blown genetic mutation.

Bruce's movie posters are on my walls, all over Chinatown, in every record store, and in the head shops on Yonge Street. Above all, he's in my head. Thinking about him without staring off into space can be hard. My teachers catch me sometimes. I wouldn't want Baba to. He'd tell me to stop horsing around and get back to work. My sister would laugh if she knew and blab it to her friends. My mama? Who knows what she thinks. No, we Chinese men can't be like that. We can show satisfaction after a good meal, be pissed when the Leafs lose, complain about not having any money or about our parents. But no, getting soft is definitely not an option.

Chapter 7

Gwai Lo Girl

My best and only friend, Andrew, in 12-C2, would probably think talking to a man who's been dead for four years is nuts.

When I was a kid, I used to write to another super-mutation—Dave Keon, the greatest Toronto Maple Leaf ever. He was such a big hero to me. Now, it's a tie between him and Bruce. Keon had to leave Toronto because the pile of crap from the owner was so high it could be smelled in Japan. He suffered in silence. Why should I? Bruce went out doing what he loved—making kung fu movies.

Andrew says that, at eighteen, we can do almost anything. I can vote. I don't need parental permission to drop out of school or join the army. I could take off on my own. But I wouldn't. I basically run the restaurant. They need me, and everyone knows it. Why would I leave, anyway? I'd only wind up working in another restaurant. I don't have the mutant DNA strand.

One morning, I was on the grill doing the Red Pagoda's Kodiak breakfast special—grilled cheese with a razor-thin slice of barbeque pork, half-priced if you came in wearing Kodiaks. That was my idea. Students and construction workers lined up in the morning for them. After several complaints by people who didn't wear Kodiaks, we made it half-priced for everyone. Baba made us use day-old bread to cut costs, which wasn't a bad idea.

I had other great new ideas—a lunchtime loyalty program (the twentieth lunch is on us!), combo plates where customers get a meat, a vegetable, and fried rice, plus dinnertime delivery with a three-dollar minimum (before taxes).

Buying that greasy spoon was Baba's brainwave and probably his worst. The joint came with broken ventilation, mice, and heavily armoured cockroaches. Mama went apeshit when he bought it.

Things were slow, so I pulled out my copy of Leon Uris's *Trinity* and got into it until a fresh breeze chased away the usual sticky, heavy smell in the restaurant. I turned around, and a hot girl twirled her hair and asked if I went to CTS. That's Central Technical School.

I'm sure my face turned red. It was Angie Dehaut from the grade-twelve arts program. Angie da Hottie, we called her. At CTS, there are like twenty guys for every girl, so we recognize all the girls. But unless you play on the football team or have a boss ride, you don't stand a chance with them, especially if you're me.

"Do not think." Bruce jabbed a finger into my head. "Do. How many times do I have to tell you? Be yourself."

"Shut up," I said.

Angie looked around. "Who are you talking to?"

25

"No one. How can I help you? I mean, yes, I go to CTS."

She pointed to a pack of cigarettes. The fact that she'd recognized me from CTS was primo, better than having a supply teacher all day.

Bruce stood behind her, flexing his muscles and puffing out his chest. "She is pretty, Johnny. Make a move. Eliminate your ego. Do it, ask her out."

I took a deep breath and straightened up.

"Are you okay?" she asked.

"I'm in 12-D4," I mumbled. I emphasized the *twelve*, so she'd know I was in grade twelve and wasn't some punk junior FOB Hong Konger, just happy to be here. I'm a Canadian, and I run this joint.

Bruce slapped the back of my head. "Nothing wrong with people from Hong Kong."

"You were born in San Francisco, you're American," I reminded him.

"Okay, some Hong Kongers are okay."

Angie's forehead crinkled. "Who are you talking to?"

"Sorry, I was just reciting a passage from the book I plan to use for a report."

She looked at my copy of *Trinity*. "My mother's reading that. My dad's Irish, so she said I should read it. I'll take those smokes, please."

I was so focused on how her ivory skin flowed from her neck to her collarbones that I plunged into highly restricted territory. I fantasized about picking her up at school with a new Datsun 280Z. I'd gun the engine and shout to all the other guys, *See ya, suckas*, and they'd be so envious.

"Hello? ... Peter Jacksons?" She sounded annoyed.

I reached for the smokes but felt her studying me, dissecting me with her eyes. I squirmed in my skin as though I'd been called out at a school assembly for not being able to grow a moustache. I wished I'd stuck to my morning routine of sit-ups and knee bends, put on a cool shirt, and got my hair cut.

I handed her the smokes. "Anything else?"

She shook her head.

Some gum so that your breath will be clean when you kiss me.

"Okay, that's $1.10." *It's free if you become my girl, and we hold hands at school.*

She winced at our overcharge for cigarettes and pulled out a two-dollar bill. I pushed the bill back into her hand and tossed a few fortune cookies onto the counter. "On the house."

"Right on, I love these." Her eyes lit up at the cookies. "Peace out."

My eyes glued onto her knee-high boots and tight jeans as she walked out.

Baba walked over wearing a rumpled white undershirt, his face unshaven. I hoped Angie hadn't noticed him and figured him for my dad. That would be so embarrassing.

"Johnny." He whipped me with a tea towel. "Stop giving away our profits. What's the matter with you? You have no time for that." He snapped his fingers. "Besides, I will find you a wife ... a strong worker. You two will be my managers." He chuckled, but he was serious.

He would be okay with me working more shifts instead of going to school. He thinks someday he'll run a chain of restaurants, and I'll be his right-hand man.

Why couldn't my baba be cool? He's not much older than Bruce was when he died. Well, that's not true. My parents are dinosaurs at forty.

I said to Bruce, "Your mother was part gwai lo—Dutch and English, wasn't she? Hard to tell in those old black-and-white shots."

"That's right," Bruce said as he did two-fingered push-ups.

"Then you went white, too, and married Linda Emery—and kept the tradition alive."

"I've always had a thing for white meat." He jumped up and showed me some skin, all while smiling big.

"Stop talking to yourself," Baba said. "No one will want you if they think you are strange."

I wanted to tell Baba I could find my own wife, just like Bruce had. Maybe Angie Dehaut will be like Linda and marry a Chinese.

Chapter 8

The Meatheads

MY FAVOURITE PART of every morning is writing on the Red Pagoda's sidewalk sandwich board. I write out the day's special alongside a different saying with coloured chalk I hide from Jane. I do poetry, quotes from books, as well as some religious stuff I fool around with, like:

> *God helps those who help themselves to good Chinese food.*

I've been playing with some of Bruce's pearls of wisdom. Today's was:

> *Life itself is your teacher, and you're learning so long as you eat Chinese food.*

Jane stormed down the outside stairs from our apartment above and entered the restaurant from the rear. She grabbed breakfast then paused to read the sign before offering an unwanted opinion to piss me off.

"You know, if Bruce Lee were around, he'd smack you upside the head for messing with his sayings."

I told her to piss off, like I do every morning, and then we got on with our day.

But each day after school, my sign is defaced with little kittens and cutesy images of flower power and girly stuff. I recognize Jane's work, but she denies it, the little shit.

I always hide the chalk in a different place before leaving for school, sometimes in the most obscure and impossible-to-discover spots, like behind the buckets of grease or between the coffee filters. Yet she finds the chalk, and messes with my sign.

The cat-and-mouse with Jane over the sign has become part of our routine. The sign also brings in the occasional walk-in, and just as importantly, it allows me to write and share it publicly, even if it's only a line or two a day.

Mama finally shuffled in from our apartment upstairs after the morning service. She poured herself a coffee and sat at the only round table in the restaurant, a table we'd nicknamed "the living room."

Baba looked at his watch and asked if the traffic had made her late. I know Mama didn't appreciate the sarcasm. He then gave her heck for not staying away from Auntie. I'd heard this all before, but never understood why Mama was supposed to stay away.

Auntie was the first woman ever to run the gaming side of a Wong Association and likely the first woman in any Chinese association. Mama once mentioned Auntie yearned for full status at the table with the executive board and would do anything to get it. Rumours had started going around that she was associating with the triads, the same gang supposedly behind the restaurant bombing. She's tough and means business, but a goon? No. I can't see Auntie kneecapping someone. That's bullshit. People run her down because she's a woman. Whether it's true about her triad links or not, I'll bet it makes debt collection easier. Still, I wouldn't want to find out.

Mama lit a cigarette and took a heavy drag. "Go to school, Johnny."

I couldn't tell if she wanted me to leave or stay. Maybe she didn't know, either. I should've been at school already, it was eleven a.m., but instead I'd stayed up last night to drag her out of the Association and now was doing her breakfast shift. She looked terrible: bloodshot eyes, a dishevelled ponytail. Deep, erratic sighs between heavy drags of her cigarette. I wondered how she felt about me bailing her out. She was risking our restaurant and our home.

I almost repeated what Auntie had told me, that she wasn't going to be covering Mama's back anymore. But Baba was nearby, and if he heard, they would scorch the earth with another epic couple's fight. It would also fuel Auntie and Mama's cold war, so that Mama would be fighting on two fronts—again.

Instead, I told Mama we didn't have anyone else to work the floor, and it was pushing noon anyway.

"Go to school." It sounded like a plea, as though my leaving would lessen her screw-up. "That is your job. Your baba and I will run things."

Honestly, they suck at running things. But I let her shoo me away, and I tried to make it to the end of my second class.

With its collegiate, gothic-style architecture of hand-cut stone, gargoyles, and silver marble inside the front doors, Central Tech looks like a university. I figure my fancy high school is as close as I'll get to a real university. Central Tech is big enough to build airplanes, fix a fleet of cars, and teach more than two thousand students. Girls used to have separate entrances and stairways leading to their floor where no dudes were allowed. I guess our "Industry, Intelligence, and Integrity" motto was missing a fourth *I*—"Include girls."

The smokers and stoners hang out along Harbord Street. They cluster around the pinball arcades where Andrew and I often meet after school. Most people in the arcades—me included—rarely look further ahead than the next smoke break.

The school secretary ignored me as I signed in late. On my way to class, one of the teachers shoved a boy up against the wall—just another day at CTS. No one bothered to slow down. The school year's only two weeks old and feels like a life sentence.

The lunch bell had rung, so I went straight to my locker to dump my books and ran into Andrew. He always has sad, puffy eyes like he's just woken. He towers over me in the platform shoes he wears year-round. His hair flows down to his upper chest, with his bangs pushed to the side like his hero, bassist and frontman Geddy Lee of Rush. It's not hard to pick him out of a crowd. He might have a chance of scoring with girls if he at least faked liking disco or the Rolling Stones. His wild look is pretty hip. But he doesn't care. I've never known him to try hard at anything except changing a timing belt.

His dad runs a garage on Portland, off Queen. Once, I helped them work on a Datsun. I didn't do much, but we fixed it. Then, we took a smoke break and cracked some beers.

Like me, Andrew's expected to remain in his parents' orbit. I assume he'd be happy to work with his dad after graduation. They work in perfect synch, seamlessly sharing tools and space. Unlike Baba and me, they seem comfortable around each other. I've never shared a beer with Baba. He's only interested in me when he needs something or if he thinks I've done something wrong.

A picture of Andrew and his dad hangs on the wall in the Szymanski garage. Andrew was probably about eight or nine in that shot and looks cute handing a wrench to his smiling dad. When I was that age, Baba was AWOL.

When Andrew's dad left to make a phone call, Andrew opened more beer.

"My dad's the best mechanic there is," he said. "He wants to make me partner—'Szymanski and Son.'" He stretched his hands out like he was holding a sign.

"Right on," I said. Although, to me, that sounded like the Polish equivalent of a life sentence working in a Chinese restaurant.

"Except," he said, "sometimes I think he just wants me close. His old man was killed in the war, and he thinks he needs me to be around." Andrew had told me about his family history: the Warsaw Ghetto Uprising, how his parents met in a bread line, then again in Montreal before they moved to Toronto.

"The thing is, what I want is a garage that specializes in vintage rides, like a '55 Bel Air or a '57 Thunderbird. Man, I'd love to work on stuff like that. Dad isn't interested in the classics."

This was my first time hearing Andrew talk about the future. I was jealous that he had a dream separate from his family's.

I tried to sound enthusiastic. "That sounds great."

"Yeah, and you can deliver me lunch on Fridays and payday. If you don't skimp on the portions, I'll give you a decent tip."

It took me a second to realize he was joking.

Students buzzed around us in the wide hallway. Andrew, towering over me, suggested we go to Tony's for a slice and a smoke.

The hallway was a stadium of acne-infected spinning tops who'd been trapped and forced to sit through geography, French, and Canadian history all morning. Now, with fifty minutes of freedom, they were exploding with joy. They slammed locker doors, yelled friendly profanities across the hall, and turned the silver marble floor of the rotunda into a football mat.

"Here comes your new best friend," Andrew pointed into the crowd.

Baahir, a student from Pakistan who'd arrived before the last school year ended, rounded a corner with his head and shoulders down. He's one of the tiniest students in the school and easy to miss. We aren't sure if he can understand everything we say in English. All we get are head wobbles. We share classes, and he follows me everywhere, even sitting beside us in the caf, with his lunch, which always looks and smells pretty interesting.

He mostly stares at the floor in his Honest Ed's bargain-bin clothes. If there were a social ladder to climb, talking to him would easily cost me a few rungs. I'm not far from the bottom already, so I can't figure out why he follows me. Andrew's told me to tell him off, but I can't. Maybe that's why he hangs around.

He dodged several clusters of students until he ran into the twins Domenic and Pasquale, a couple of meatloafs built like concrete blocks, who play for the senior football team.

"Here, Paki, Paki, Paki." Domenic pretended to hand off a football to him and told him to run.

Asshole. Calling Baahir that word was like dropping three stun grenades, as mean as any slur on the planet. I wanted to drop a spinning heel kick to Domenic's teeth.

Baahir smiled awkwardly and then lowered his head. But that didn't stop the meatheads. They laughed, and then Pasquale's foot came out, tripping Baahir, who fell onto his face. His books scattered and his tin lunch box spilled all over the floor, drawing laughter from those around him.

"Anybody smell curry?" The meatloafs jeered and then moved on like conquering heroes.

Bruce came up alongside them and cracked his knuckles before levelling round kicks that passed through their heads. He looked at me and squinted. "Stupid jerks. Take them out." He jabbed.

I shook my head. It was so easy for him to say that. "What am I supposed to do?"

Bruce dropped low and shot his leg out to trip the meatloafs. I followed suit and took Pasquale's leg out for real. He fell hard. People chuckled, but he got up fast and spun around with an accusatory glare, shutting everybody up.

I tried to look innocent, but his eyes rested on me. "You stupid chink." He shoved me hard into a locker, drawing *oohhhs* and smiles from students around.

I swear it was like a *Lord of the Flies* moment happened—they formed a half circle around Pasquale and me, chanting, "Fight, fight, fight ..."

"Kill him, Pasquale."

"Cover your nuts. Remember their sneak attack at Pearl Harbor?"

"Crush that grasshopper."

I was too scared to say or do anything. I knew I was going to get my head kicked in. What had I been thinking?

The assholes egged me on, pretending to do Bruce's moves and shrieks as if I were a carnival sideshow. I wished I had some nunchucks or even just some basic fighting skills. I had fear and anger, nothing else.

There are times I cringe at what Bruce has done. Sure, he kicks ass and stands up for people, but now people think we all do that. It's like that's the only way to gain respect. At that moment, I resented Bruce and wished it was still the gentlemanly Dave Keon who was showing me how to walk away and take one for the team.

"Leave him alone," Andrew said, working his way through several students. But then Domenic said a slur about Poles and shoulder-tackled him.

Pasquale grabbed my shirt and pinned me to the brick wall. He smelled of Irish Spring and cigarettes. I remembered how Bruce was a rebel and hated traditional dogma. He said street fights were about getting out alive, not being pretty. I looked for something, anything. Pasquale's jacket protected him from bites, but his Adidas provided no protection for his toes. I stomped on them. He swore and grabbed his toe, releasing me. I pushed him into the crowd and ran straight into Mr. Miller, bouncing off him like a pinball off a bumper.

"To the office, now. Both of you." Vice Principal Miller grabbed Pasquale and me.

Chapter 9

The Fish out of Water

PASQUALE AND I weren't the only students waiting on benches for Vice Principal Miller. Pasquale leaned into me and said if he got another suspension I was a dead man. I almost shit myself but played it cool by pulling out a copy of *Hamlet*.

Bruce never bothered with soliloquies. He just went in and showed them who was boss.

"That's right." Bruce practised roundhouse kicks in his Kato outfit. "I would have taken Pasquale's head off before he even had a chance to blink."

"I'm not you, and besides, you were pretty useless for me back there," I said.

"It's you who must train and work harder. You must adapt and find your purpose. Then you can stand up for yourself and other people."

"I said I'm not you. I can never be you. No one can." I hoped I didn't sound too whiny. It didn't matter how many sit-ups I was up to. Measuring myself against him was like trying to outrun a tiger.

"You won't fail if you accept yourself and stop trying to be me," Bruce said as he flipped over and did a shoulder press.

When Bruce starred in *The Green Hornet*, it was the first time we'd ever seen martial arts done by one of us on an American show. They wanted him to fight American-style. He refused.

"Right again," he said, ripping off his jacket and flexing his biceps. "I fought my way. No one was going to tell me what to do. I had to slow my moves down because the camera couldn't keep up. That gave me the idea to use blurry movements in *Fist of Fury*. It was psychedelic." He waved his hands around in slow arcs.

Mr. Miller came out and called me into his office.

"Johnny Wong, 12-D4 ..." He directed me to a chair and sat behind a big desk cluttered with files. He flipped through some papers. "You have all your credits ..."

As he read, he bit into a sandwich. Mustard dripped onto my file. He swiped it with a finger and smeared it back onto his sandwich. "You aced all your academic courses, although your shop marks have historically been weak—aircraft mechanics, 62; machine shop, 64; chem, your major, only 63. This is also interesting— you miss exactly five days and a couple of half days each year, all parent-approved." He looked up from my file. "Coincidence?"

"Allergies and family matters, sir." I forged all my parents' notes, and their signatures on my report cards, not that my parents cared. Andrew and I skipped and went to the movies during those half days.

He put the papers down. "Johnny, I know you write the year-end anonymous editorial in the *Blow* each year."

That's our school newspaper. Mr. Miller had been my English teacher until his promotion to vice principal this year. We used to talk about books, not just the assigned readings. He knew how I wrote and what I read. "So what, sir?"

"Johnny, last year's piece about police brutality was so well written that it belonged in a real magazine. The year before, you argued against the death penalty. And the year before, you crafted a well-rounded parable about capitalism." He paused and stared at me.

"No one else in the school can string together thoughts and arguments like that. I presumed you were going for a *Go Ask Alice*-type thing, anonymous notoriety."

"*Go Ask Alice* is about the diaries of a teen druggie. I don't do drugs, sir, and neither do any of my friends."

He threw his arms up in mock surrender. "So let me ask you. What are you doing here?"

"Pasquale pushed me into the—"

"No, Johnny, that's not what I mean. However, tangling with Pasquale Ciancio wasn't very bright. What I mean is, why are you in this school? What are your plans? Where are you going?"

I couldn't tell him that I came to CTS because I thought it would be easy and that I wanted to follow what few friends I had at the time. Beyond that, I had no plans.

Bruce had dropped out of the University of Washington and opened several martial arts studios. I'd say he did alright without school, so maybe I didn't need it either.

Bruce sat cross-legged on the carpeted floor in his varsity jacket, chewing on a blue ballpoint pen with a spiral notebook on his lap. "Johnny, school might not have been for me at that time. But I met Linda at UW there, and I have always been open to learning and expanding my mind."

Mr. Miller took a phone call.

"You scored big with Linda," I whispered.

"That's right." Bruce released a big grin.

"Is it true American girls are smarter, richer, and more sophisticated than other girls?"

He rested his chin on his knuckles in deep thought. "Basically, girls are the same everywhere. They like sports cars, action movies, and men in fancy clothes. You must also say nice things about their hair, nails, and body. Don't worry, you'll learn. Oh, you must also be funny. They always like the funny guy, even if he doesn't shower." He smelled his armpits and grimaced.

"That's what I thought." I did a behind-the-back skin with him.

"What did you say?" Mr. Miller said as he put the phone down.

"Nothing, sir."

He placed his sandwich down and wiped his mouth, smearing mustard on his sleeve.

"My point is you're an academic floating through a technical school. You're in your last year. You have some decisions to make."

I blinked and dug my shoe into his worn carpet.

"What do your parents want, Johnny? For you, I mean?"

I hesitated. "To work at the restaurant, sir?"

"They own a restaurant?"

I nodded. "The Red Pagoda. Free delivery on orders over three dollars."

"On College, near Bathurst?"

"Yes, sir." I didn't tell him that table eleven, our only round table, is our "living room" when it's not busy. It's where we sit, wrap wonton, and snap green beans while doing homework. It means that even separated by the street entrance and back entrance to our four-bedroom walk-up apartment upstairs, we can never escape our restaurant's sounds and smells. I also said nothing about Mama and Baba sleeping in separate beds when she's not crashing at the Association or wherever.

"Oh, so your parents took that over." His smile dropped. "I've passed the building many times. What is it, about thirty seats?"

"Twenty-four, including the counter stools, sir."

"Hmph, it's the third attempt at a restaurant there in six years."

"We're different. We deliver." Even though we had the same cracked cement floors, the same chipped melamine counter, the same chickenshit-yellow walls, and the same blackboard with daily specials posted of whatever we had to get rid of. I'd convinced my parents to put a TV above the coffee maker for customers, which Jane took over if there was a program with Shaun or David Cassidy on.

"That's great. We often order takeout. Do you have beef with bitter melon?"

I was impressed that he knew the dish. "Yes, sir, my mother makes the best."

"I wish we had done career planning before. Working at the family restaurant is fine, but is that what you want to do?"

That was a silly question. What I wanted didn't matter. I was in a Chinese family. I was good at helping run a restaurant, looking after things, and getting people out of trouble. I was one of several interdependent ingredients essential to the whole. You stay put, or the whole dish falls apart. I shrugged.

Mr. Miller studied me like a complicated metaphor. "Have you thought about college?"

"College, what for?"

"Journalism, creative writing?"

Bruce read philosophy and wrote books. Could I? Mr. Miller seemed to think so. I have to admit, it intrigues me the more I think about it. Then, I imagine Mama sleepwalking through her shift. They need me to make sure breakfast gets off the ground, that the kitchen prep gets done, deliveries made, the stock ordered before and not after we run out of things. And I have to keep an eye on Jane. What a joke: go to college to get a job that doesn't make money. Plus, it costs money. Who'd pay? Even if we had the money, it could never happen.

"Johnny, you're a fish out of water. Do you copy?"

I played innocent, but I knew what Mr. Miller was saying, and it was the same thing that's been slowly infecting my thoughts. This is my last year of high school. What am I going to do?

"You're doing alright here, and I bet you run that restaurant as well as you write. But maybe you can do more. I've got a friend who's starting up the writing program at West Connecticut. Your shop marks bring your average down, but he believes in giving other voices a shot. You'll have a chance once he sees your academic scores and some of your writing. Let me put in a word for you."

I didn't know what to say. Was "other voices" a good thing for once?

"Just think about it, Johnny. You could be a writer instead of a waiter."

That hurt. Then he told me I owed him a lunch detention for the scrap with Pasquale. He advised me to stay clear of the guy.

I left the office, avoiding Pasquale, who was chatting up a nursing student in her whites. Students shuffled back to class from lunch. My stomach growled. Out of the corner of my eye, Baahir snuck up on me. Without looking up, he handed me a Twinkie, a stick of Bazooka, a packet of Pop Rocks and a bag of crunchy Cheetos, my favourite kind. I guess you could say I've started to warm to him.

Chapter 10

Working Man

Throughout the afternoon, I thought about what Mr. Miller had said. *You could be a writer instead of a ... waiter.* Writing, what a stupid idea.

After the dismissal bell, I avoided Domenic and Pasquale and went to Tony's Pizza and Arcade to meet Andrew. He likes Tony's over the other three pinball joints on Harbord across from school because the pizza's decent, the games are easier, and they sell single cigarettes, ten cents each or three for a quarter. I like it because there's rarely a fight in there, unlike Manny's or Nick's, where the jocks and stoners hang out.

I had about twenty minutes before work. Andrew moved gingerly as he navigated between students in the crowded arcade. Domenic had tackled him hard.

I thanked him for trying to watch my back earlier, but he waved it off like he always does. Nothing really fazes him. The only things that excite him are fixing cars and airbanding Rush songs.

Andrew said, "A rumour's going around that Rush is returning home for a couple of days to see family and check out a new studio." He told me he'd made a bull-shit call to the recording studio in his best deep voice and asked when Geddy would be in so he could deliver a new amp pedal. They told him October 31.

"So?" I said.

"Call it the Halloween Rush. That's perfect. Come on, let's get down there. We're gonna hang with Rush and get them to sign my albums. I'll borrow my dad's camera and we can take our picture with them."

He jumped into airband mode and started to sing "Working Man," one of Rush's singles, which is all about working and not having time for anything else. His enthusiasm is infectious, and the song speaks to my life, but I had to pull a downer: I said I'd probably have to work.

"Book it off, man. We'll skip, you're being an old fart." Andrew always wants to do stuff together. He likes cruising in his firetrap Pinto up and down Yonge Street. He wanted to see *Star Wars* again and tried to get me to go with him. I feel bad that I'm always saying no. I guess I'm pretty lucky he hasn't given up on me. I have to give him that.

"Okay, I'm in." I tried to sound enthusiastic.

An unfamiliar voice came out of nowhere. "My father says Rush is a pale imitation of Led Zeppelin."

Andrew and I turned around to see Baahir.

"Oh yeah, what do you think?" Andrew asked.

Baahir kicked the floor and then shook his head. "Rush has a progressive sound, more like Yes and King Crimson. But the complex storytelling is dreamy. I can't get enough of *A Farewell to Kings*. I want to go with you, please," he said, eyes downcast.

Andrew and I exchanged incredulous looks. I said I was cool with that.

"Sure, man, let's do it. Johnny, tell your parents you have a project at my place or something. It's time for you to have some fun."

Chapter 11

They Call Us Bruce

AFTER SCHOOL THE next day, I chatted with some students outside Nick's while I waited for Andrew. They said they loved Bruce in *Enter the Dragon*. Of course, they did. Everyone did. But only I knew him. "Sometimes I wish you were a nobody," I told Bruce. "Then I could have you all to myself."

"I was a nobody. Let me tell you, it's no fun. Now, I am happy to be there for anyone. Why? Because everybody deserves an opportunity to develop."

"But everyone talks about you like they know you."

"Let them. They are nothing compared to the Hong Kong media sharks. To them, the only thing worth knowing is gossip. The only thing worth doing is selling newspapers. Truth is meaningless."

I don't like talking about Bruce with gwai lo. They don't get that he was not just a martial arts master. He did everything. He wrote his own scripts, directed, produced, and acted. He bent the rules and took control of his life. Plus, I hate how gwai lo think we all have a martial arts gene. When people feel that way, I usually smile along because I don't want to be that guy who doesn't know how to have fun.

Baba and I loved Bruce in *The Green Hornet* and some *Batman* episodes. He was the best fighter there and could take anybody down. Then we saw him on *Longstreet*, which, as much as I loved *The Green Hornet*, was his best role.

"Thank you, Johnny," Bruce said in the same red-and-white striped tracksuit he wore in one of the *Longstreet* episodes.

"You didn't mind playing the hired help to another rich white guy?"

"Of course, I minded. But the director also let me be myself in some scenes, and I got to talk about the philosophy of Jeet Kune Do. There is nothing more gratifying than being who you are." Bruce did several quick front snap kicks. "The *New York Times* said, 'The Chinaman came off quite convincingly.' My episodes were the best in the series. We would have been renewed if they hadn't slotted us against *Ironside*. I would have been even bigger." He beat his chest. Still, I knew Bruce could do more and better.

"That's right," he said. "Everyone must fulfill their potential. Mine was returning to Hong Kong to make movies my way. I also had two kids to feed and was almost broke."

Back in 1973, in grade eight, Baba took me to the Pagoda Theatre in Chinatown to see Bruce's first movie, *The Big Boss*. That was before we owned the restaurant. No Jane, no Mama—he called it a guys' night out. He bought popcorn and snuck in cans of Coke and White Rabbit candy. Bruce became the one thing Baba and I shared that was fun and exciting. We talked endlessly about him. We played and fought using his moves and his sounds. We flexed our muscles and pretended to lick our blood the way he did.

Baba and I also did a guys' night out for his other movies. It became our sacred ritual. This was before US theatres released his movies and unleashed him onto the gwai lo. It was like Baba and everyone else in the packed theatre were a family with the inside track on a secret: a private audience with our very own kung fu God.

We cheered when Bruce took out Chuck Norris in *The Way of the Dragon* and when he fought the drug lord in the mirrored room in *Enter the Dragon*. Man, that must be one of the greatest fights ever.

When it came to Bruce, Baba and I were linked.

Then, when Bruce died suddenly and mysteriously, it ripped an entire race's guts out. He was the first and only Chinese to become an international star. He didn't play demeaning Charlie Chan, Hop Sing roles with buckteeth and Chinaman accents, bowing to everyone. He had attitude and swagger. He walked with his head up, kicked butt, and did it for all Chinese. So, when he died, Baba lost it. He didn't lose it like he just got a parking ticket but like a part of him was taken away.

Baba was very suspicious. He read and reread all the newspaper reports about Bruce's sudden death. For weeks, that's all he talked about. No external injuries were found. Poison was suspected. If only that Taiwanese actress, Betty Ting Pei, had found him sooner. There were rumours she was his mistress. I think that's crap. Linda showed honour and respect at his funeral. Maybe the triads did him in? Or maybe it was an ancient curse?

The Hong Kong newspapers talked about drugs and orgies. Again, more crap. Some said it was heatstroke because it was the hottest day of the year, and he was training and working like there was no tomorrow.

Things got worse when Linda took his body back to Seattle for burial, far from his most loyal fans. So many people were upset. Conspiracy theories ran rampant. Protests and bomb threats in Hong Kong forced the British colonial government to investigate, led by a forensic expert.

"The Americans, maybe they killed Bruce," I said to Baba. "You always say they can't be trusted."

"Could be, could be." He stubbed his cigarette into an overflowing ashtray and folded his newspaper. "They screw everybody."

"Or the Russians, they're rivals to be leaders of the communist world, and they hate the Chinese."

Baba thought hard about that, too, then shook his head. "You know who hates the Chinese even more?"

"The Nazis?" I had just completed a project on World War II, and Nazi world domination was on my mind.

"No, no. But there is a link, an Axis, you might say." He grinned like he had a dirty secret.

We shouted in unison: "The Japanese!"

I smacked my forehead, and Baba pretended to beat me with his newspaper.

"Of course ... the Japanese—the enemy."

Every Chinese person has a story of the invaders during the war, which started long before Hitler crushed France. My grandparents ran from the Japanese when they overtook their village, sending them into hiding. They starved in hiding. Baba had a twin who died of malnutrition as the Japanese bombers destroyed everything and terrorized everybody. We still think they're barbarians. Baba even has a thing against "those ugly Japanese cars." He said they'd never sell, and you'd never see a Chinese person driving one.

My mama joined in on one of our anti-Japanese rants one time. She scoffed at the thought of eating raw anything, especially fish. "The Chinese are sensible and cook everything, even lettuce," she said.

I'll bet the Japanese run their mouths about us, too. Everybody needs a bad guy.

Bruce's second movie, *Fist of Fury*, is where we first saw him use nunchucks to beat the snot out of the bad guys. Afterward, every Chinese kid hounded their parents for them. When Baba returned after all those years, he gave me a pair, but Mama forbade me to use them. It's also the only movie where he chose to die.

"That's right." Bruce flexed his biceps. "With a battle cry, I jumped into the firing line of the Japanese army rather than surrender. Why? Because I wanted the power of martyrdom to restore Chinese honour and dignity." He stood tall, clenched his fists at his side, and puffed his chest.

It was Mama who told me about Baba's twin. Baba never talked about his past or what was in his head. It's like a force field between us. Bruce made that go away. More so than the Leafs ever did. Baba doesn't love them as much as I do. It's too bad, because I think Bruce and Dave Keon are equal in the hero department. If I could deliver to only one house, I don't know which of theirs I would choose.

Baba and I were closest in those days. But it was also bizarre. After him being away for years, I didn't know how to be his son, and he didn't know how to be my baba. He got me things to play with but never played with me. He was always working. Plus, to be honest, I was suspicious. I always wondered why he left and if he'd leave again. Nobody ever said anything, but it was obvious: he'd had an affair with another woman, and that's how I got stuck with Jane.

So, Bruce was our glue. Then, the British forensic expert published his report. He said it was "death by misadventure." That sounded like Bruce had fallen into a hole while looking for treasure. People got even more suspicious. The expert also reported it was a reaction to a painkiller and Aspirin. Nobody believed that either, but just in case, no one took Aspirin for a while.

"White people killed Bruce Lee," Baba said. He licked his thin, cracked lips. "He was getting too popular, so they put him in what they think is his proper place—beneath them."

That's about the only time Baba ever said anything about prejudice. He told me to forget about Bruce, that I had to get busy. After that, he never said much to me, and when we got the restaurant, there wasn't much else for us to talk about besides that. You'd think we'd connect over that. But it's his dream, not mine. Maybe that's why I'm bitter about working in the restaurant, even though I'm good at it.

Now, if Baba learns about Mama's debt, even Bruce won't be able to save us.

Chapter 12

Barry's Back

IT WAS MY night off, so I avoided the restaurant after school and ran straight upstairs to my room. Then Mama called me down.

"Jane has a math test tomorrow. I'll do the kitchen, you drive tonight."

Math was like breathing for Jane. She was going to ace it even without studying. I said it was so unfair that I always had to work, while she got another free pass.

"Please, Johnny, why do you keep complaining? Just do it. You are her big brother. You must lead by example. Your baba thinks she could be a doctor or a lawyer."

Or a psycho. We all know she's Daddy's pet. From how Mama asked, I knew that saying yes would mean one less fight between her and Baba.

Jane came down for a snack and made a big deal of her hard work and her need to study. Then she winked at me and twirled her hair as she turned on the boob tube for *The Hardy Boys/Nancy Drew Mysteries*.

I've always wished we were an average family, like *Little House on the Prairie* or *The Waltons* normal. I never watch those shows, but I'm certain John-Boy never had to deliver sweet-and-sour pork. Mama and I used to play mahjong together, watch reruns of *The Green Hornet*, go out for noodles, and even hang out with other families. Not anymore. I'm also not a kid anymore.

I wouldn't always have to smell like a deep fryer if I just said no to working. Then what would I be? I keep thinking of Auntie's job offer. I bet she pays well. I remember when Auntie and Mama used to try to get along. They'd make each other fancy dishes, bring out the Johnnie Walker, and exchange gifts. Mama even gave presents to Leo. Then, out of nowhere, it's World War III between them. I could hear them arguing behind closed doors about parenting and what everyone would say. All Mama ever told me was that they came from the same village and lived together when she came to Toronto. I hate not knowing what I'm missing.

Since we bought the restaurant in '74 when I was in grade nine, we're only together as a family when we work. That's when Mama started taking off, usually to the Association.

It was a quiet night, so I looked at my math homework. I thought about what Andrew had said about me being a boring old man. Was I really? I'm eighteen; that's not old, and that's exciting. I can vote, I can marry—not that I care to do either. I can drop out of school. I can see an R-rated movie. What else is there in life?

"Johnny, stop daydreaming. Three combos, 105 Robert Street, Unit 1." Baba placed a delivery order on the counter before me.

The Vega stunk of Baba's cigarettes. I opened the window and fiddled with the radio dial, landing on an update on the Leafs' training camp. Captain Darryl Sittler is expected to have another big year. Plus, Ron Ellis is coming out of retirement. I'm pretty sure it won't be long before they win the Cup again, finally, after ten long years. Even now that Dave Keon has left the team. It seems that everyone I care about leaves at one point or another. Now, it's hard to follow Keon's games because nobody else cares about the WHA and his new team, the Hartford Whalers. I get depressed just thinking about it. I wish I'd gotten to see him play before he left.

Bruce and Keon have so much in common—both are smaller men. Keon, like Bruce, moves with grace and speed, able to explode and pounce on an opponent's weakness. Anybody could tell he loves what he's doing. Watching Keon is like watching Bruce, who never trash-talked or showed up an opponent. Keon bleeds honour and dignity, too, just like Bruce did.

Bruce sprung onto the hood of the car, wielding a hockey stick like a halberd, ready to decapitate a horde of bad guys. He said, in response to my line of thought, "Not only that, Jeet Kune Do is about integrating mind and body. I am sure your ice-hockey friend would say the ice and stick are parts of his body as well. I would assume that only by playing hockey was he at peace."

He threw several hockey pucks at a mailbox, embedding them like ninja darts, then leaped off the car and disappeared.

I turned onto Robert Street, right behind Lord Lansdowne, my old middle school, looking for number 105. Parking in front of it, you could tell it was an Italian or Portuguese neighbourhood. They love their iron gates and fences and stone walkways. Grapes hung in bunches the size of footballs. Statues of Jesus with arms outstretched.

I rang the doorbell several times until a goateed guy my age with golden hair and a menacing stare opened the door, releasing a cloud of pot. Through bloodshot blue eyes, he said, "What the ... Johnny, Johnny Boy, my man?"

It was my old friend—Barry Arble.

Chapter 13

Destiny, Man

HE TRIED TO hug me, but that was awkward, so we slapped each other's hands.

"We got the serious munchies, so this better be good," he said.

When Barry and I were in Mrs. Stover's grade-five class, he lived at the corner of Henry and Baldwin. At one point, after he pulled me out of a garage fire that psycho Jane started, we were both in separate foster homes. Yeah, that really happened. He'd jumped back into the flames for my sister but collapsed unconscious. That's when Rollie, a friend of mine at the time and Mama's main squeeze back then, came to the rescue. The burn scar is visible down Barry's thick neck. Barry's ripped now, chest muscles making his shirt even tighter. One time back in grade five he called my dad a slut, so I sucker-punched him. There's no way I could get away with that now.

He was partying and invited me in. I said I only had a minute and followed him down a narrow flight of uneven stairs. Two girls stood over a record player, listening to a Peter Frampton song.

They turned around. One was Black, and the other was Chinese, which was weird because it made me think of Jane hanging with guys like Barry. Baba would freak out for sure.

"That smells good," the Chinese girl said as she nodded toward the food.

Barry handed the bag to the Black girl. "My girlfriend, Ayeisha. Johnny here's my best friend from back in the day." The other girl was Shelley, who cleared off a table strewn with *MAD* and *Cracked* magazines.

The girls dug into the combos while Barry bit into an egg roll. "Yo, this is primo. Remember your mother used to bring those weird balls of meat when I was in the hospital?"

I nodded. Sui mai, har gow. Mama wanted to shower him with gratitude for saving her two kids, so I didn't have the heart to tell her he had thrown them all out. My parents still talked about him sometimes as our saving hero.

Barry had been in and out of CAS care, and I hadn't seen him in five years. I sent letters to him when he was in juvie, but many were returned unopened.

I didn't know where to begin or what to say. An awkward silence descended until he told a couple of bad jokes. "Why are Italians such good magicians?" He was already laughing at his punch line.

I shrugged.

"Because they can make people disappear." He cracked up.

He told another bad joke, one that made me wince. The girls' reactions didn't show much. I guess they were used to him. I changed the subject and asked where he went to school.

"School?" He laughed. "I haven't been in like two years. The last school I went to was Danforth Tech. They were going to kick me out, so I dropped out. You're still going?"

"Yeah, CTS." I wanted to ask what he was doing instead, but I thought that might make him feel bad.

"A lot of stoners there, right?"

"Yeah, but I don't really hang with them."

"Maybe you should."

I didn't know what he was getting at. Instead, I told him how great it was to see him, and I meant it. Back in the day, we hated each other at first, but it's true—he became my best friend for a while.

He showed off the rest of his basement pad, a big room with a half wall separating the small kitchen from the rest. He had moved in a few days ago. He flashed his new stereo: Technics turntable, tuner and speakers, real quality stuff. He had a rocker recliner. His TV was no big deal, but he said he would get one of those monster twenty-one-inch Zeniths soon. We have a nine-inch black-and-white in the restaurant. Suddenly, I was sorry to have run into Barry.

"You mean it's yours, you live by yourself? What about your family?" As soon as I asked, I regretted it. He didn't live with his family when we were kids, and I shouldn't have assumed things would be any different now.

"My mother and sister got a crib somewhere in Scarborough. Or no, that was the last place. It could be Moss Park now. Dad went back to Cape Breton. So, this is all mine." He nodded as he opened up a Styrofoam container of noodles.

Barry's situation feels more familiar to me than Andrew's. Andrew's tight with his dad. They may have different dreams, and his dad came through a war, but they've got it together.

The girls continued to pig out as Barry explained that the Children's Aid booted him out after he aged out at sixteen, but they still give him a monthly cheque. It's not enough, so he does some roofing in the summer and snow removal in the winter. But he told me he's sitting on a great opportunity to score some serious coin. He didn't say how, but it sounded big.

He grabbed a beer for me and lit a joint. It worked its way through the girls and then to me. I waved it off, saying I had to work, although I sipped on the beer. I'd never smoked up before. Who knows what's really in that? I've heard about weed being laced with LSD or angel dust.

We chatted about our days at Orde Street Public School and our old neighbourhood.

"Remember Barb, our CAS worker?" Barry asked. "You had the serious hots for her, man." He explained to the girls that we had the same social worker and were in foster care.

"You?" Shelley's look was accusatory, as though I'd shamed our entire race, our ancestors, and everyone to follow.

I averted her stare. "Yeah, Barbra Twomansky. I was ready to marry her at eleven years old," I said.

The girls laughed, and Barry cracked up.

"Then she goes and throws me and Jane into a foster home after a big fire that almost killed Barry."

"I heard. But he came out looking shagadelic." Ayeisha fondled Barry's neck scar.

Barry tensed his biceps and chuckled.

"So, Barb and I were done after that," I said.

They laughed again. I figured their weed high made me funnier.

"I can't even remember most of my foster homes," Barry said. "All I remember is trying to run away to find my mom."

Barry never used to say anything bad about his mother. Nobody in care likes to go negative on their parents and nobody ever said how they got there or why they couldn't go home. If parents cancelled visits or didn't show up, we'd pick a fight with the social worker who put us in there or the foster witch who kept us there.

Gladys, my foster mother, was alright. But nothing could have been more humiliating for our parents. Imagine having your kids taken away and made to live with strange white people. Years later, Jane teased me at dinner when I dropped my fork, saying it reminded her of when Gladys tried to teach me how to properly use the knife and fork. Mama and Baba unleashed simultaneous death stares on her, silencing that topic forever.

Gladys looking after us confirmed something I tried not to think about but knew in my heart, even then— our parents totally sucked at raising us. It meant I'd have to do it myself, and I would have to look after them, too, if I wanted us to stay together. It became my mission, even if I was stuck on autopilot. In a way, it worked with who we were. Plow everything back into the family. Throw everything into respecting and protecting Baba, Mama, and our name. It was very Chinese, and I liked them needing me.

Barry'd had to play it differently. Anytime he got comfortable and settled, he got moved, or his mother returned, all cleaned up for another go-round. Eventually, the CAS gave up on his mother, but he was too old and wild to get adopted by that point, so I guess things were worse for him.

It didn't take long for his basement to become a haze of smoke.

Barry cranked up the music. He sparked up another joint, took a huge hit, and blew the smoke into my face, which made the girls laugh.

"Come on, Johnny, let's party!" he screamed.

Ayeisha said Frampton was lousy dance music and put on "Money, Money, Money" by ABBA. That got them grooving. He waved me on.

Barry sparked another joint, took super tokes, and then chasing me around the apartment and exhaling at me like a game of tag. I looked at my watch and saw that twenty minutes had gone by.

"I have to go," I yelled over the music.

"What?" Barry stumbled with a beer in hand.

I'd finished my beer and was feeling pretty mellow just standing there.

"I have to go. I have other orders to deliver." That was true, but my life suddenly felt shitty compared to his. He has his own pad. He has girls, music, money. Baba'll get me a dutiful bride from China who'll do a great job managing the restaurant while I drag Mama away from the Association again and again.

"Don't leave, man. I'll put on some Cheech & Chong. We'll laugh our faces off." He leaned into me. "We can party it up with the girls."

I shook my head and made for the door. Barry walked me out and slipped me a joint. "Sinsemilla, for after work. It'll knock your socks off."

"Thanks, man." I handled the joint like it was a bomb. I was too embarrassed to say I'd never smoked up. After all, who wants their gonads to shrink?

"There's lots more, way more." He glanced around to ensure no one was listening. "There's so much that I need help moving it."

I looked at the joint, then at him. "What are you saying?"

"I'm saying, Johnny Boy, I know why you're here."

"It's kinda obvious. You're wasted, and you've got the munchies. It's a lucky coincidence for both of us."

"No, man, it was meant to happen. It was destiny." Barry dug his fingers into his head like he was into ESP or something. "Everything has a meaning. It's all part of a master plan. There are no coincidences, can't you see?"

"Man, are you ever stoned."

"No, I mean yes. It doesn't matter. I get it. You were brought to me. I have this amazing opportunity. But I just couldn't figure out my next step. You're my next step. You're the only person I can trust. We can make some serious coin together."

"What are you, crazy? That's like trafficking. I don't know anything about selling this."

"I'll bet you run that restaurant like a Corvette Stingray. You were always smart."

Mr. Miller had said something like that, too. But I didn't feel smart. I knew I'd be delivering combo plates for the next forty years.

"Running a restaurant and pushing drugs are two different things."

"They don't have to be. Hey man, just try the weed. It will sell itself once the word gets out. Easiest money you'll ever make, swear to God."

I shook my head. "Where'd you get it, anyway?"

"It came to me like you came to me. Never mind where. Think about what you can do with the money, man."

It was a crazy idea. He was asking me to be a criminal. It would mean humiliating my family and destroying my future. But then again, I don't have a future. With the weed-business idea, paying Auntie off and going to college might be possible.

Barry jumped on my hesitation and gave me his phone number.

"Think about it, Johnny Boy."

Chapter 14

The Earworm

> *When opportunity knocks, knock back . . .*
> *some delicious Chinese food.*

The idea came from the earworm Barry put in my head: *Just think about what you can do with the money, man.*

We might lose the restaurant if Leo and Auntie meant what they said. Baba will leave after that. He always talks about how good things were in Vancouver. He'll probably take Jane. I'm not sure what Mama and I will do.

The day after hanging with Barry, at dismissal, I was packing my bag by my locker when I saw Mr. Miller steaming my way. He's a bloodhound when it comes to finding skippers and drugs. I realized I still had the joint Barry gave me. Crap. He stopped right in front of me.

"We need to talk."

He was using his serious vice principal voice, the one he used when he went from class to class with the police and sniffer dogs.

"Me?" I reached into my pocket and fingered the joint, ready to ditch it in the crowded hallway.

He nodded.

My hand dug deeper into the pocket, two fingers wrapping around the weed. "I didn't do anything." I felt a bit weird after Barry's, but I hadn't smoked anything. And all I was carrying was a joint. Could I get expelled for that?

He leaned toward me. "It's about your future, Johnny."

I pushed the joint into a corner of my pocket. Several students casually dropped f-bombs until Mr. Miller turned, raised his voice, and silenced them. He returned his gaze to me and said, "Now, where was I? Before I forget, do you deliver as far north as Dupont? We're south of there."

"Huh?" I didn't know what to say at first. Finally, I said yes, but it came out as a question. How was this about my future?

He smiled. That's when I figured things were cool.

He peered into my locker and scanned its contents. "Most guys have pictures of Suzanne Somers, Farrah Fawcett, Wonder Woman ... you have Dave Keon in his Leafs jersey and Bruce Lee."

I used to have more pictures of Bruce. I got sick of everyone being goofy and pretending to do martial arts with me.

Bruce leaned against a locker in a CTS varsity jacket, cradling textbooks under his arm. "You have a quarrelsome mind. Unless you learn to calm it, you will never hear the world outside."

I'd heard that before. "*Longstreet*, episode two?"

"No," Bruce said, "the pilot episode. I had so much fun making it."

Miller's face creased. "What are you talking about?"

"Dave Keon is still a Leaf, sir. The best ever," I said.

"Agreed. Have you ever seen him play?"

I shook my head, embarrassed to say we never had the money or the time to go. By the time we did, Harold Ballard, the evil Leafs owner, had driven him out of town.

"Hmph. Then you will like what I have to say. Did you consider our conversation the other day about West Connecticut State?"

Connecticut seems so distant, like the kind of place rich white kids would go, ones who don't have combos to deliver or families to referee. Yet Bruce crossed an ocean alone to America for high school and college, so why couldn't I go to Connecticut? But no, so long as we have bills to pay and food to deliver, I can't imagine it.

"I don't know, Mr. Miller. It's a long way from home, and my parents need me."

"It's about as far as New York City from here, but closer to where you want to be. I spoke with my friend there. We discussed your writing, your schoolwork, your family situation. He wants you to apply, and so do I."

I wasn't expecting that. "But it will cost money ..."

He handed me some pamphlets and forms. "Info on tuition fees, books and supplies, housing, grants and scholarships. Think about it: you could be the next Michael Crichton."

I've seen Crichton's novels while browsing bookstores. He's the most famous bestselling writer today. But who's going to publish something with my name and face?

"And you know who else is down there?"

I shrugged.

"Dave Keon, that's who."

I looked at his picture. Of course. He played out of Hartford, Connecticut.

It was like Mr. Miller read my mind. "It's an hour and a half from the college. I know because my buddy and I saw the Whalers play the Jets—Bobby Hull! Can you imagine Dave Keon and the Golden Jet on the same ice? I was there. Do you copy?"

"Wow, for real?"

"And here's the good part, Johnny, I paid eight dollars for a ticket three rows back from the Whalers' bench. I could hear Keon psyching up his teammates like a captain. They're practically giving tickets away. They don't appreciate hockey like we do."

"Are you trying to psych me out, sir?"

He clenched a fist and grimaced. "I wouldn't kid about that. Somebody should shoot Ballard for letting Keon go and not letting him back into the NHL."

I enjoyed seeing that side of the vice principal.

"Johnny, promise me something."

"Yes, sir?"

"Whatever you have to do to see Keon play, do it. You won't regret it. It will be the experience of your life, trust me. Connecticut is your best chance. Heck, West Conn is so close, you could be a season's ticket holder at those prices."

I bit my lip. It sounded like a dream come true. I could even cover those games for the school paper. But who was I kidding?

"Whatever you have to do—do it." His face softened. "Don't worry about your parents right now. You focus on the application and your grades. Deadline is

February 1." He handed me a form. "I expect it to be completed before the Christmas break."

You'd think he was sending his son to school and getting the basement back the way he smiled at me. I didn't want to disappoint him and said I would work on it. The thought of seeing Dave Keon play made my head spin. But college, journalism, writing—it sounded incredible. Is it possible? How can I make this my future?

Whatever you have to do—that's what Mr. Miller said.

Chapter 15

The Scholar on the Run

ANDREW HAD TO help his dad with a transmission job, so I headed home. Before I stepped off school property, Barry, standing by a tree, waved me over. He took a final drag of a cigarette before crushing it. He wore the same tight T-shirt that showed off his muscles, tattoos, and scars. Students gave him room the way you would someone who'd just been released from jail and wanted to bust you in two for no reason. We gave each other skin like old friends. I hoped other students were noticing that I hang with someone who looks like a badass, and I wondered if we'd become good friends again.

"Did you try the smoke?"

I felt the joint humming to life in my pocket. "I didn't have to. I know it's good stuff."

We took the long, slow way to my place, going along Harbord and up Robert. We stopped in the schoolyard of Lord Lansdowne to hang off the monkey bars, eventually sitting on the swings.

"How long have you and Ayeisha been going out?"

"A month. She's a fox, ain't she?"

I whistled in agreement.

Barry chuckled. "Johnny Boy, you wanna ask me about Shelley, don't you? Tell me you don't want to jump her bones. Unless you're a cherry boy." He dropped me his goofy laugh.

"What, me? No way." No guy wants to admit that he's a virgin.

"That's my man. Let's get you some real action. You don't want to be wasting it by jerking off all day and night. It's not good for you. Let me set you up with her. She's your kind, and you two would make a great couple."

I cringed. Why did he have to say it like that? Yeah, I noticed her, like I do every girl. I'll bet Bruce did, too.

"She's single." Barry gave me a playful elbow. "Every time Ayeisha brings her along, she's alone. Drugs open doors, man, and girls follow."

I would rather he got me a shot at Angie, even though I don't have twelve-inch biceps.

I told him I couldn't be any less interested in Shelley because she reminded me of my sister, which made me want to vomit. He laughed and said he'd like to see Jane again.

"Don't even think about it." That came out louder than I intended.

He scoped out the yard, pulled out a joint, and sparked it up.

I looked around and wanted to say that wasn't a good idea, but I didn't want him to think I was a complete dork.

He exhaled and then passed the joint to me. He said it was the same killer smoke from the other night.

I took the joint but said I had to do deliveries later and couldn't be high doing it.

He called me a nerd and dropped that goofy laugh again, like he was holding a low musical note in his throat. "Shit." He jumped off the swing. He looked to each end of the yard, back and forth. Men were approaching from each end.

"Cops, swallow it," he said.

"What?"

"Swallow the goddamned joint."

I hesitated. He pulled the joint out of my hands and gulped it. "Run like a motherfuc—" He tore off through the playground toward one of the high chain-link fences and started climbing. One of the cops went after him. The other one flicked away a cigarette and charged after me.

"Stop right there," the cop yelled.

I bolted off the swing and headed toward the portables, but there was no way out. I ignored my pounding chest. If I got caught and arrested, my parents would freak out. If it messed with my graduating, for sure, I would be doomed to deliver for all eternity. I took a deep breath and remained still. I expected the cop to cut me off at the far end of the portables. I'd guessed right. I ran toward the end of the yard vacated by the cop now chasing Barry.

I was off the school grounds in an instant and continued running. I glanced over my shoulder and saw one of the cops drag Barry off the fence. The other cop ran onto the sidewalk after me. I tore up the street all the way to Harbord before stopping and looking back.

There was no sign of Barry or any police. I had run many blocks, faster than I thought humanly possible, zigzagging through side streets like Barry and I were still ten and playing *Rat Patrol*—dodging cops who weren't there, hiding behind cars and mailboxes. I remembered how much fun that was.

I made it to the restaurant just as fumes were drifting out of the kitchen, causing customers to cough. Mama and Baba were in the kitchen, yelling at one another.

"What's going on?" I asked.

"Your baba buys a restaurant with broken ventilation and blames me. How is it my fault he is a bad business-man?"

"We would have working ventilation if you hadn't blown our profits. If someone calls the health department, they could close us down. Johnny, you're late." Baba handed me an order pad and instructions to bring a plate of dinner to Jane. He told me to get the meal to her and then take over the floor while he worked on the ventilation.

But they weren't done fighting. They're never going to be done. They boxed several more rounds, going back and forth like two punch-drunk heavyweights. I heard Baba tell Mama to stay away from "him." Who did he mean? Is Mama having an affair now, too?

It took a while before things quieted down. I called Barry a few times, but there was no answer. I tried again at the end of the evening, and he picked up.

"You okay, man?" I asked.

"Yeah, I'm cool." He laughed as he told me the cops couldn't bust him since he wasn't carrying anything. "I had a half bag of weed but ditched it before they got me.

The pigs didn't see anything. That didn't scare you off getting in on some action, did it?"

I paused long enough for Barry to think I'd hung up. I imagined us losing the restaurant, my family splitting off, and us never being together again, not even for a final mahjong game. It wouldn't be like flunking machine shop if I failed at selling weed—it'd be so much worse. I'd lose the only thing I was known for and really good at. I couldn't even be the invisible Chinese delivery guy anymore. That's how low I'd fall.

Students would gossip about me if I got caught. They'd say they knew I was a loser and that I got what I deserved.

But there could be another narrative where I don't get caught. It could end with me making big money. I could pay the loan off without Baba finding out. Mama would be pissed at first, but how could she not be happy? War averted—peace on earth, debt gone. We wouldn't fall apart like a dumpling spilling its entrails. And maybe there'd be something left for me, like college.

"We've had a lot of fun before, Johnny Boy. We can have it again while making some serious coin."

"Uh-huh."

"Uh-huh, what? Man, if you don't get in on this, I'll have to call the Children's Aid—what with all the hours you and Jane put in. There must be some child-labour law you're breaking." He laughed.

"No, that won't be necessary. I'm in."

Chapter 16

The Deal

BARRY SAID WE had to be careful about what we said on the phone since the fuzz already knew him from some B&Es, which to me sounded paranoid. He suggested we meet "where the Catwoman used to live." I knew that was code for Henry Street.

We met after I did a round of deliveries. I parked at the top of Henry and walked down the street, looking for Barry, stopping in front of my old house, number 56. Somebody had bought the place and sandblasted the brick to make it look new and fancy. It didn't look like a rooming house anymore.

I passed Meany Ming's old house, which her son had sold. Beside it was Catwoman's place. Mama had told me she moved out a few years ago. I felt bad that I never saw her after we moved to the apartment above the restaurant. Out of habit, I looked around for her Maine coon cat.

Barry startled me by jumping out from behind a tree. "Jesus, Barry, you scared me."

He laughed his goofy laugh and gave me some skin.

We climbed a fence and took the laneway to McCaul Street, then onto Orde Street, our public elementary school. We then sat on the see-saws in the empty playground.

"I wonder if Mrs. Clover still teaches here," Barry said.

"Dunno." I shrugged.

Barry's tone shifted. "Let's talk business." He said my share was 25 percent, that the restaurant would be the distribution centre, and that he'd bag nickel, dime, quarter, and half-ounce bags.

I was impressed he'd done some thinking.

"You got somewhere in the restaurant you can hide the stash?" he asked.

"In the restaurant? You want to turn the Red Pagoda into a drug depot and my family into criminals?"

"Heck no. They won't know a thing."

"How much dope are you talking about?"

"You mean the whole stash?"

I nodded.

"Five pounds, minus some quality-control sampling here or there." Again, with a goofy laugh like his, it was a puppet show.

Who knows what five pounds is worth? Is that even a lot? I thought of the basement behind the furnace, then realized going down there all the time would draw suspicion. "No, this isn't going to work."

"Why not? Once I hand out samples, this will be a piece of cake."

"So that's your plan, just send people to the restaurant? What kind of a ridiculous plan is that?" I was no longer impressed.

"Take a chill pill, man." He lit a cigarette. "It's only for a short while, maybe a couple of months."

"Really? How do you figure that?"

"Because I know what people want, and this stuff is dy-no-mite. It'll sell like hotcakes, you'll see."

Selling drugs out of the restaurant could increase business, even if only a few combos at a time. But it would be the wrong crowd, and I wasn't sure it was worth the risk. "I don't like the sound of it."

"Okay, then I can restock you each night. Bring over a bit at a time."

"Sounds like I'm doing all the hard work."

"No, man, I did most of the work already. I busted my ass to score this. I'll do word-of-mouth advertising and then direct them to you. It's my risk talking to people I don't know."

I wondered how he'd scored so much dope but left that question for another time. "You don't have to handle the weed or the money. I'm assuming all the risk."

"I'm carrying samples," said Barry. "Trust me, man. I saved your life before. Why would I screw you over? Besides, I figure you kind of owe me big time."

Technically, I was unconscious when he rescued me, and I'd had no choice. But the scars on his neck were visible reminders of my debt to him.

"How much bread are we talking about here?" I asked.

"If we only sold by the ounce—around twenty grand. But the demand for nickels, dimes, quarters, and halves is always high. It's easier to shorten those counts and maybe walk away with twenty-five. We're talking serious coin. I wasn't bullshitting."

I'm sure my eyes just about popped out. "Are you kidding? That's insane."

"Damn straight, it is. I wasn't kidding about making serious dough." He made it sound as though even in a worst-case scenario of having to sell it in large quantities, my 25 percent take would be huge.

"That's a take of at least five or six grand for you. Yeah, I know some math, dude." Barry read my mind.

I was speechless. That was beyond anything I could imagine. That would pay off Auntie, get us some new ventilation, and, for now, anyway, bring peace to the family. I could buy the new Atari 2600 and even get a tracksuit. That and a scholarship might be enough to get me into college.

But Barry didn't have much of a plan. Holding all that pot, having stoners come in and out of our restaurant, Mama would get suspicious for sure. It also meant I'd be a junior partner.

"Partnerships can be messy," Bruce said, jumping onto the climbing bars and doing one-armed chin-ups. He hardly ever partnered. When he did *Enter the Dragon*, he went in as a team but did his own thing, not having to rely on anyone.

"He's not very smart, is he?" Bruce stopped his chin-up midair.

"I didn't say he was stupid."

I got off the see-saw and pinged a few pebbles off the slide as I bit into the inside of my mouth. "No, this isn't going to work," I said to Barry.

"C'mon, man, you said you were in." He jumped on the monkey bars and did some fast chin-ups where Bruce had been a moment before.

"I still am. Except," an idea was forming in my mind, "they'll be deliveries—special deliveries."

Barry raised an eyebrow and dangled from the bar. "What?"

"We don't sell hotcakes, but we do sell egg rolls. They order egg rolls. Every egg roll comes with a dime bag. We'll create an egg roll special: Buy six bags, get one free. That's a quarter ounce, seven grams, right?"

He swung back and forth on the bar before landing in front of me. "What if someone wants an egg roll?"

I worked it out like a math equation as Barry lit a smoke. "We separate real orders from pot orders. Pot customers have to ask for it with ... mustard, a packet of mustard on the side."

"Mustard? Like a code."

"Yep. Start me up with ... five ounces divided into dime bags. I don't want it inside." I knew the rafters in the garage behind the restaurant would be the perfect hiding spot.

Barry's forehead scrunched. "That's a lot of little bags."

"How else were you planning on doing this?"

His silence confirmed that he hadn't thought it through.

"Okay, what if our customers can't remember?"

"They'll have to. It's a one-word code—*mustard*."

"What if you're not working?"

"I'll take extra shifts. But I need Monday and Tuesday off."

"Days off? You can't shut down. What if someone needs a hit?"

"We're already closed on Mondays. Besides, if we limit availability, we create more demand."

"What?"

"Imagine if *The Bionic Woman* was on only once a month."

"What, really? I just got used to them moving it from Wednesday to Saturday."

The same night as hockey. I remember having to make that difficult choice about what to watch.

"No, just pretend for a second." I knew Barry couldn't tell if this was a joke or for real.

"Man, there would be street riots if they did that." His mouth dropped.

"It would be awful, for sure. But people would circle that day. Everything would revolve around it. The network would be on fire. The streets would be empty."

"I get it. I get it now. Keep them desperate. Build excitement."

"Let's try it."

He agreed. We worked out a few more details, like when we'd meet and how we'd pass off the weed and the money.

That evening, Leo surprised me at work as I was closing up. He scanned the room and asked if we were alone.

I nodded.

"I don't want to say too much, but you have to cough up some dough soon," he said.

It had only been a few days since I spoke with Auntie. I had hoped for more time. "I have something in the works. Just give me a few more days, and I'll deliver. Promise."

"Johnny, I could have gone straight to your parents. I'm doing you a big favour. You don't have a few more days. Your loan's going to be called in. This is serious, man."

For someone who had come to collect on a debt, Leo looked more concerned than menacing. But I sensed he meant what he said. All of a sudden, Barry's talk about quick money sounded urgent.

"What can I do to buy a week?"

"A couple hundred might do."

I emptied the cash, handing Leo $120. Then I ran to my room and the sock drawer, pulling out another eighty bucks.

"Will this do it?"

"We'll find out."

Chapter 17

Drug Lords

GETTING INTO BUSINESS with Barry reminded me of Bruce's first movie, *The Big Boss*, where the bad guys used their ice factory as a front for drug smuggling. Bruce kicked their asses. Does that make me the bad guy here? Would Bruce kick my ass, too?

"I'm not sure I could, Johnny. You're up to what, twelve push-ups? You would be a tough out, and how you handle the nunchucks—I'm scared just thinking about it." Bruce chuckled.

"Shut up, I can do twenty."

He recoiled in jest.

"You're supposed to help, not mock me. And how the hell am I ever supposed to learn to use nunchucks without banging my forehead with them every fricking time."

"Perhaps they are not for you. Adapt what is useful, reject what is useless, and add what is truly you. Explore. You will soon discover what works." He flexed his arms. "Plus, the ladies will love it."

"But I'm not trying to be rich and score with the ladies, although that would be nice. I just want my family to be a family. I want them to stop fighting all the time. I wish we weren't in debt. This is not a career move."

"You are taking a big risk. Are you sure this is who you are?"

I shook my head. How could I know who I was? All I really know is what I'm supposed to do. But I can manage the risk. I'm hoping that dealing will be like mahjong—see what you have, make a clear plan, remain discreet, think before you move, and watch everything that's going on around you. That's the stuff that Auntie taught me. You have to be good to be lucky. I'm ready to be nimble like Bruce and quickly change strategies when necessary, like stopping if the cops start snooping around.

Barry came to the restaurant on Sunday. He sat beside me in our living room and handed me a big sandwich bag filled with a bunch of smaller ones. It was weird the way those baggies made everything real. I was now a drug lord.

"Barry Arble!" my baba called out. "What a surprise. Johnny didn't tell me you were in touch."

Baba asked how he was. Baba insisted on cooking him some special dishes. Barry said he had some errands to do. But when my mama came out and called him their lucky white star and insisted he stay, he was stuck. Years after the fire, Barry was still a hero to my parents.

The scene reminded me of all the Japanese monster movies and even the Chinese ones I'd seen as a kid. All the locals would be running around scared as hell. Then, the one white guy would step in with all the answers, and everyone would stop and wait for his wisdom because he always saved the day.

Bruce's movies were different. He always played the reluctant hero. The only white guys there got their butts kicked.

"Just eat and run. They love you," I told Barry. "Like, where do you have to be, anyway?"

Barry looked around and whispered. "I'm sitting on a dozen pin joints I plan to spread around Yorkville, Yonge Street, the university, wherever people are looking to score. We're in business, remember?"

"Mama, make that to go. Barry has to leave," I yelled into the kitchen.

Barry smelled something he liked and walked into the kitchen. "That's okay, Mrs. Wong, I have time for a quick visit and some of your delicious cooking. It's nice to see you."

Like Eddie in *Leave It to Beaver*, he was always smooth with my parents. He wolfed down his dinner and got ready to leave with some takeout menus to hand out. As he stood, Jane bounced in after her piano lesson.

"Jeepers creepers, is that Jane?" Barry's face lit up.

I looked at him and then at Jane, who closed in fast. "She's fourteen, Barry, and a pain in the ass. Plus, fifteen will get you twenty."

"You just said she was fourteen."

Jane smiled as she hovered by the living room table. "Aren't you Barry?"

"In the flesh," Barry replied.

"Holy cow, you've been working out." Jane gawked at Barry's muscles. He sat back down, and she slid beside him, eyeing his burn scars. They chit-chatted about what, I don't know or care, but I didn't like it.

"Barry, you need to get going," I told them both.

After forever, he left with a promise to Jane to return, leaving me feeling queasy.

It was a quiet evening. Really slow. I had the boob tube going with *To Kill a Mockingbird* on. Would Gregory Peck defend me if I got busted? I imagined he'd take my case not out of pity but because he smelled an Oscar.

He'd have his thumbs firmly planted into his vest pockets and say: "The Oriental gets out of life what he deserves, no better, no worse." He'd shake his head at the travesty of justice. "Your Honour, my unscrupulous but well-intentioned Oriental was simply trying to protect his family from fellow yellow hordes. Almost anyone would be capable of such a crime under his circumstances." I'd whisper to Atticus not to say *yellow horde.* He'd lose like in the movie, so I'd lose. However, he'd be hailed a martyr for defending the little yellow guy, whose name would be forgotten but who should've been grateful just to be there.

We closed early and sent the dishwasher home. I guessed Barry didn't have any luck. The plan was for me to phone him if I sold anything and then hang up. That was the signal for us to meet in the parking lot of King Edward Public School after work. But no egg roll with mustard orders came in, just the usual combo plates. What if he got robbed or, even worse, arrested? I was starting to realize how risky this is.

Barry didn't answer the phone. I walked up to King Edward to see if he was there, but no luck. I walked to his apartment. It was dark and quiet. I wanted to knock, then remembered what he said about the police watching him. So I went home feeling like the world's worst drug lord and barely slept.

Chapter 18

The First Delivery

I WAS REALLY glad to see Barry under the same tree after school on Tuesday.

"Why didn't you check in? I've been trying to reach you for the past two days."

He said giving out samples was a piece of cake, except he wound up toking with each potential customer. He got so baked that he fell asleep at Ayeisha's and partied all of the next day. He's supposed to be a partner. What if he gets hurt or busted? What if I need him?

I get how some sampling is necessary and looks good. He told me everyone loved the pot and would be calling soon. I wasn't so sure. I was pissed at him. I wondered if he was still high.

When I returned to the Pagoda, it was quiet. Baba came over with a few slips of paper. "We have two deliveries. Where are the car keys?"

I looked up. "Already?" We don't usually get delivery orders so early.

"Four egg rolls, 14 Kensington Avenue. A second order of two #3 combos with one egg roll, 234 Madison.

The first delivery is a funny one. Our delivery charge is more than the food."

We charge twenty cents per egg roll. I hid my excitement and shrugged. "They like our egg rolls."

"With mustard." Baba chuckled. "With both orders? That is different."

"Baba, I can get this. Take a break while things are quiet."

"No, I want to get out. We also need a few things from Chinatown."

I jumped out of my seat. "I'll get it. I mean, I need to get out and clear my head. Driving helps me focus."

"Since when?" Mama joined the conversation from behind the counter. "I know you, Johnny. You hate driving. You hate delivering. What is going on?"

"Nothing."

"Johnny's got a girl, I bet," Jane said out loud.

I shot her the dirtiest brother-to-sister look.

Baba pointed a finger at me. "You have a girl?"

"Sure, he does. He's been moody all week. She probably hasn't returned his call. Johnny's got a girl, Johnny's got a girl." The little shit giggled.

"Son of a gun," Baba said as he punched me in the arm. "Is she Chinese?"

"Are you a boob or butt guy?" Jane giggled some more.

God, why couldn't I still be an only child?

"Jane, stop," Baba said. "That is so rude and unnecessary. He is still your dai goh, and he is my son, so obviously, he prefers both butts and boobs. More importantly, what does her family do?"

Jane and Baba gave each other some skin.

I turned to Mama to rescue me.

"Stop this." Mama glared at them before turning to me. "Do not do anything to humiliate us." She brushed her index fingers together and cracked a smile before unloading a tray of cups.

Jane and Baba snickered. I've never had a girlfriend, so no wonder they were excited about making me squirm.

"You have to treat them like fine porcelain," he said, straight-faced. "Delicate and beautiful. Remember, the most fragile cups can carry the hottest tea."

"What does that mean?" Mama asked.

"I don't know," he said, smiling. "I read it in a fortune cookie."

They laughed at me.

I grabbed the delivery slips, Baba's grocery list, the food, and the car keys and headed for the door.

"Remember, don't pop your zits on your way there," Jane yelled out.

"Wear a tighter shirt, son, and do some push-ups."

Mama joined in. "Make sure she's Chinese!"

My first-ever drug deal was at a Madison Avenue house just west of Varsity Stadium. Two girls in U of T sweats opened the door right away. They tipped me well and were so friendly and happy to see me that it made me think college might actually be fun. It made me hope every weed run would be that easy.

I swung down to Kensington Avenue for the four-egg roll delivery and found parking nearby. I grabbed the stash of baggies under the passenger seat and pulled out four dime bags. I slipped them into the food orders, stepped onto the row house's short porch, and rang the bell.

No one answered, then a man in an Argos cap stepped out and from the side of the house. "Red Pagoda with the golden herb?" he said.

I nodded, then whispered, "Forty dollars, four egg rolls ... with mustard."

He asked if it was all there, including the egg rolls. He winked and then handed me a small bundle of bills. As I unfolded the money, he grabbed the bag and walked away. I looked at the bundle of bills: a two-dollar bill wrapped over some newsprint. He ran off. I tore after him. He was fast, but I was faster. He ran up the street and almost piled into a rack of vintage clothing put out by Courage My Love. He then turned into a narrow opening between some row houses. Just as I was gaining on him, a guy built like a brick house stepped out, blocking the opening and stopping me in my tracks.

"This here's private property." Beefy arms crossed his chest.

Mama has always nagged me to be safe. She still says "stranger danger" because of twisted creeps like Ted Bundy, the Son of Sam, and the killers who murdered that Portuguese shoeshine boy, Emanuel Jaques, off Yonge Street. It's like she wants me to believe there's a murderer behind every corner. What if she was right this one time? I hesitated to look behind to see if someone had trapped me, but I twisted my head and saw a clear route to daylight on the street. I tore out of there and jumped into my beat-up Vega.

I'd been set up. Every delivery guy gets robbed like that. It's like falling off your bicycle when you're learning.

But this felt different. It wasn't some guy wanting food. It was druggies scoring weed. I checked for smashed car windows. Sometimes, thieves'll try to break into your car when you're on delivery to a bogus address. Luckily, most of the five ounces were still under the seat.

I drove around to let off some steam. Maybe dealing wasn't for me. But what would I say to Barry?

We met in the yard of King Edward Public School. He said the robbery was on me, that I should have been more careful, and that I had to make up for the loss. That pissed me off. I said he'd smoked up some bad dudes and that he was responsible for finding better customers.

"I could have been killed."

He shook his head. "Take a chill pill, man. Nobody's gonna kill you over four dimes."

He was right. But I'd been terrified back there.

"And what if you're lying?" he said. "What if it never happened?"

It didn't matter how much bigger Barry was. I squared my body to him. I might be a drug dealer, a bit of a smartass with teachers, and I haven't returned Andrew's *Playboys* like I said I would, but I am not a liar or a thief.

"That's right. He crossed the line," Bruce said with narrowing eyes. He tore off his jacket and beckoned Barry to come at him. Bruce took a flying leap into Barry, going through him as Barry lit a smoke.

"Screw you, Barry. You know I can be trusted. Why would I lie?"

That made him think, but it was like he was paranoid. I know weed can do that, just like it fries your brain cells and makes you stupider. How do you run a business if your partner thinks you're stealing? No wonder Bruce always worked alone. I told Barry I was ready to quit.

He saw how upset I was and agreed to share the loss fifty-fifty, but this would be the only time.

"No, that's not enough." I put on my blank mahjong face and demanded a third of every order. "Take it or leave it."

"You rat bastard. We're partners. We had a deal."

"Well, partners are usually fifty-fifty. And if one partner walks away, the deal is over. You're still getting two-thirds without the risks that I have every night. You get high, I get robbed. What kind of partnership is that?"

He wasn't happy about it, but we shook on it because we're friends.

Before he got famous, Bruce used to have to do crummy jobs, like washing dishes, and he hated teaching kung fu to rich movie stars.

"It wasn't that bad, really," Bruce said. "I liked Steve McQueen. He was a buddy. He's an angry, intense man until he trusts you. But afterward, we were cool. And James Coburn was peaceful and calm. He understood the philosophy of Jeet Kune Do."

"Still, it feels like we have to put up with a lot of gwai lo shit, don't we?"

Bruce nodded and opened a copy of Descartes. "I refused to put on pigtails and play a coolie. That would've paid some bills, but it would've been degrading."

Chapter 19

The 49ers

Two FOBs around my age came in early in the evening and gave the restaurant a slow look before taking a booth. I dropped two menus and recited the daily specials. One of the dudes was big with puffy cheeks. He could've been a Laughing Buddha, except for an awful perm and a losing war against acne. He rolled up his sleeve as he picked up the menu. I recognized the characters for the number forty-nine tattooed on his forearm, signifying that they were triad soldiers—shit.

Everybody's been whispering about how the triads blew up that restaurant on Elizabeth, the one that probably fell behind on payments, about how they run protection and most of the gambling houses and even pay off the cops. I've heard they're moving into drugs. It might all be overblown bullshit. The papers make it sound like we're all shifty and dangerous; however, the papers also say that the police are so concerned, they've formed a special Chinese unit.

I know the uncles distrust the police. Some mahjong games are repeatedly busted, whereas others are left alone. That makes me believe that some of the police work for the triads.

I didn't know if Mama realized who these tough-looking Chinese guys were when she took their order and chatted them up in her fast but casual Hong Kong Cantonese. She's good with customers, especially the white ones. She gets to practise her English and enjoys chatting about anything and everything. At first, I took it as her façade of customer service, since she's never been cheerful like that with us. But it also improves her mood. She's a different person on the floor. She smiles and shows humour and curiosity.

The triad soldiers were in no hurry, ordered a pile of food, and wolfed it down. At one point, Mama pulled up a chair and had the soldiers laughing and reminiscing about Hong Kong and complaining about the cold Canadian weather. Pretty soon, they were calling her "Auntie," and Mama gave them some Jell-O and fruit salad on the house. She only gives free food to people she really likes.

I could feel the soldiers' eyes on me. At one point, Buddha Boy went to the washroom and took an extended peek into the kitchen. I was sure they were there for more than eating, but I wasn't about to ask.

As I got ready to make a delivery, Mama approached me with a smile. "Nice boys. They are from my old neighbourhood."

"You do know who they are, don't you?"

She nodded. "They're paying customers. And a happy customer says nice things about us."

"Mama, they're not restaurant reviewers. They're probably Kung Lok—triad. They are not our friends."

"Fathead and Tiger Boy are nice to me."

"How do you know their soldier names?"

"They're loud, and a good owner knows their customers."

"But they could be checking us out."

"Let them. I cannot stop that. Besides, we have nothing to hide. They are more hungry than scary. Just show respect. That is what they want, and someone to watch over them, like all boys."

I shook my head. She was more tuned in to customers in the restaurant than to me.

The newspapers paint Chinatown as a den for crime —extortion, gambling, and prostitution. No one ever wants to talk about it. Even if most of it isn't true, it makes us all look suspect.

"Mama, these are bad people. Why is it so hard for you to see that?"

She looked their way. "They are also table number nine. That means they need to eat and laugh and be looked after." She dismissed me with a flick of her hand.

She picked up another order. "Gwai lo will always think bad things about us. There is nothing we can do, so why bother talking about gangs? It's better to keep quiet about them. Play nice."

"Oh really, how would you feel if I hung around with them?"

Her smile dropped. "I will kill you if you do." She walked away.

So that was it: ignore, pretend, deny, dismiss, evade, then attack—the classic Chinese bob and weave. Keep your head down—shit's going to happen anyway.

I shook my head in disgust, grabbed the delivery, and exited the back way.

Chapter 20

Nickel-and-Dime Dealer

MR. MILLER'S WRITING idea still seemed implausible. The writing I do for the high school newspaper is anonymous. I don't want people to know it's me in case they think my writing's awful. What if they laugh at me?

But then I looked at the information Mr. Miller had given me. I laughed at the cost, almost two thousand US dollars. Then, I saw that most students receive some aid and generous scholarships. Weed money as a top-up could make it possible.

Bruce got away by going to school in the US and working in a restaurant. I wondered if he'd felt like he let his family down.

"I sure did," he said, skipping rope in his unbuttoned white Henley shirt. "Even more, I felt like a loser. My father sent me away. But Peter, my dai goh, stayed behind, even though I was everyone's favourite." He winked.

So, he wasn't the eldest, and it wasn't on him to lead the family, as it is for me. Jane has it good but can't be counted on to step up. They aren't relying on her.

College is just a ridiculous idea. My parents would never agree to it. Besides, we can't all be Bruce Lee. I'm just a nickel-and-dime rebel.

Chapter 21

Mustard Packets

WE SOLD OUT of egg rolls in two days. It wasn't a lot, only about thirty. Strangely enough, customers cared about the egg rolls, too. We also ran out of mustard packets. Barry and I had never planned to get more, since we were making things up as we went along.

Barry was pretty mad because we'd still only moved an ounce. The next day, he came in and offered to work for free. "Just for the experience," he said to Mama and Baba. But I suspected he wanted to keep an eye on things or, even worse, on Jane.

My parents thought it was a great idea for him to work for us and even offered to pay him full wages. I've never been paid that.

"Don't you have a marketing-and-promotions gig somewhere?" I said to him.

Barry's nostrils flared. "It's only part-time."

"Great, what experience do you have in a restaurant?" I asked in a perky job-interview voice.

His nostrils flared again. He said he had some and was a fast learner. I doubted both.

Baba said Barry could drive.

"Great, you've got your licence, right?" I knew he didn't.

He shook his head.

"That's too bad," I said. "Well, we could use someone to run the kitchen when we're busy. That would mean you'd be responsible for inventory control, prep, the deep fryer, and both woks. You'd have to be able to handle all the stations at once—by yourself. You can do that, can't you?"

"No problem," he said.

You didn't have to be smart to see he was lying. Baba sighed in disappointment, then patted Barry on the back. "Tell you what, Barry, roll a few egg rolls with Johnny. Let's see what you can do. Either way, I'll make you a sizzling beef plate."

I waited until Baba walked away before I ripped into Barry. "What the hell was that? You can't work here."

"Why not? Your parents want me. I can convince them. They love me."

I wanted to tell him to stop being a doofus. Instead, I had him help me make some egg rolls so everyone could see he sucked at it. It worked. I had to fix every one of his. He got discouraged and left.

I warned Jane about Barry. "He's eighteen and way out of your league."

"He's a bit of a pretty space cadet. So what?" she said. "And don't tell me what to do or who I can talk with."

"Plus, he has a girlfriend, so don't waste your time."

"Like I said, don't tell me what to do." She cranked up the volume on a David Cassidy 45, drowning me out.

Our egg roll with mustard orders sold steadily for the next couple days. A dime order here or there, occasionally a quarter ounce. The dimes were a pain because they drew Mama and Baba's attention, especially if they were outside our delivery area. I told them the word was getting around about our secret seasoning, which was not a lie.

Barry travelled further to give samples—Yorkville, Jamestown, and Regent Park. I told him to scale things down, that such an area was too far to drive. Handing out free weed and getting high was the perfect job for him. As long as he gave me my 33 percent cut like he said he would, I didn't care, but I could only drive so far while making all my deliveries and still helping run the restaurant. I pocketed any money we made from pot sales and set it aside.

By the end of the first week, we'd moved three ounces. My take-home was almost three hundred dollars—a very good first week. But I calculated that we'd need until mid-March to sell it all.

I'll kill Barry before that.

Chapter 22

The Instalment Plan

I HAD AN idea to buy more time to repay the loan without either Mama or Baba finding out. As I parked at the Association between deliveries, I spied Leo guarding the door, talking to the same Buddha triad soldier who'd come into the restaurant with a buddy. The same guy Mama had chatted up.

Leo shifted uncomfortably and nodded his head before the goon walked away. Were they trying to turn Leo into a Blue Lantern? That's what they called their un-initiated recruits. He had on a new bowling shirt today. This time, Leo was Frank.

I asked him why the goon was there.

"Nothing. I'm glad you're here, Johnny. You saved me another trip to your restaurant. You have something for my mother?"

I nodded.

"Good, Mother was going to pay a visit. And if she hadn't returned with some coin, the uncles would've sent over a couple of the boys. This is for real."

"The uncles, really, Leo?" Old men in associations generally don't shake people down for debts. They don't have to. The fear of being shunned and shamed by the community is usually enough. But if he meant those triad goons when he said "boys," that meant the Association's entire house vibe would soon be changing.

"Since when has the Association worked like that?" I asked.

"Progress, man."

"For the better?"

He shrugged. "Come on in. My mother will want to see you."

The main room was quiet. Two of the uncles waved at me. Uncle Kwong's chair stood empty, making me shiver. An empty chair usually means someone is sick or dying. I chased those thoughts away and turned toward the stairs, running into Uncle Kwong.

His toothless grin warmed me like congee on a cold day. He gestured for us to sit. I looked at the stairs but could not refuse him, and we sat.

He held my arm and said in Toisanese, "You are so well-behaved. You have respect for elders." Then he broke into Chinglish. "Good boy. You good boy." He flashed me a toothless grin. It amazes me how he's lived probably sixty years here on bad English but great instincts. He unbuttoned his coat and reached into an inside pocket, pulling out a faded cloth bag. From that, he withdrew a small sachet with threads running everywhere.

He opened it, revealing a mint-condition change purse. He reached in, but instead of pulling out a quarter, he placed a fin in my palm and folded my fingers into it.

"No tell your sister." He winked.

You'd think that was funny. But I looked at his constellation of age spots and realized I had subbed him in for my real grandfather, whom I knew nothing about. Uncle Kwong was my link to my black hole of history. And him giving me five dollars was like him giving away his last possession. He probably knew he was dying. I blinked back tears.

"Are you going somewhere, ah baak?"

He nodded. "Aren't you?" His eyelids drooped, his hand trembled, and he chuckled for no reason.

He was losing it, and I didn't need this unwanted distraction.

"Go, I can see you are in a hurry with no time. Don't waste it on an old man. Time is what life is made of. Go." He nudged me on.

I felt bad, but I did have to go. I thanked him, made a huge deal of his generosity, then tore up the stairs.

As usual, Mr. Ho sat to Auntie's right. He always wore a jacket, and his hair was neatly combed and Brylcreemed. I studied the board for a few rounds. Since this was a silent, intense game—unlike the loud ones played for pennies downstairs or in many living rooms—I figured a lot of money was on the line.

I studied the table. Auntie was playing with a concealed hand, revealing nothing. The pot had to have been decent: Auntie's knuckle was uncharacteristically twitchy, the index finger on her right hand, too.

Mr. Ho shook his head, unable to decide what to discard. Finally, he threw a 9 Circle down, which Auntie picked up and then sandwiched between her wall of tiles.

She flipped them over with one smooth flick of her wrists and pronounced, "Sik wu." She cracked a smile. She'd won.

Mr. Ho slammed the table and cursed something about a woman's private parts. He and the other two players passed Auntie a bundle of bills.

"Gwo lai, Johnny." She smiled and waved me over as the tiles were reshuffled. Then she got up and poured us some tea.

I did my usual half bow but added more spice to my greeting. "Ah yi." We stepped into the hallway for privacy.

"How is business?" she asked, a cigarette hanging from the corner of her mouth.

"Good, good, Auntie."

"Excellent. Your mama will be pleased to remove this irritant between us, and I am happy to accommodate her."

"Ah yi, that's why I'm here. I have another deposit for you."

"Another deposit? Is this a layaway plan?"

"Sort of, Auntie, but Mama can't know about it."

She studied me. "I'm not sure how to explain this to the executive when she hasn't used all the extra time we've already given her?" She shook her head.

"Then just tell her you've forgiven the loan, which I'm paying back."

"No, that's bad for business. People will not repay their debts if they think I will forgive them."

"No one has to know. Mama and I will always be grateful. And you still get the loan repaid. I'll do it discreetly." And Baba will never find out, and a shitstorm will be averted.

"Your mama will not believe it."

"You could let her win it back slowly. That would encourage others to play. Just try, please." I handed her three hundred dollars. "Another instalment will come in a week."

She counted it. "Another instalment? Johnny, if you want to play it this way, the interest is three hundred a week. Your mama still owes ..." She pulled out a calculator and punched some numbers. "Including the two hundred you gave Leo two weeks ago and the three hundred you gave me on Monday, she owes the Association $4,500."

I gulped. So, the longer I take to pay, the more money I'm throwing away.

"This is lower than what we usually ask of other high-risk debts, so do not go blabbing about it. If you don't take advantage of these terms, someone else might buy back your loan and take over the restaurant. The Red Pagoda is small but has a wonderful location."

What? Who wants our restaurant? I realized then that we weren't just talking about Mama's debt.

Auntie leaned into me. "That would be horrible for your family. I'll do everything I can to hold them off. This will help, for the moment." She waved the money. "Ever so resourceful, Johnny, such initiative. But I don't know how you can repay this. Why even try? It is a waste of time and talent." She raised her chin. "Come work for me instead."

What the hell? That was the second time she's asked me that. What is Auntie up to? My parents would freak out, and she knows that.

"Think of the money. You are smart, unlike some useless fatheads." She looked at Leo, who shifted but pretended not to hear.

"Work for me, and we could make better terms for your mama's debt. She could be clear in no time."

That stopped me. She had a point. If I was going to be paying three hundred a week just on interest, I might be dealing for a long time, increasing my risk of getting busted. All it'd take would be one pissed-off stoner ratting me out to the police, and I'd be done.

But if I were to work for Auntie, Baba and Mama would never forgive me. I declined Auntie's offer for now but thanked her anyway.

"You'll change your mind later on," she said.

I walked away, then stopped and reached into my pocket. I pulled out the five dollars Uncle Kwong had given me and handed it to her.

"That makes it $4,495," I said.

Auntie's threat against our restaurant freaked me out. Why go after us? We're small potatoes. When I returned to the restaurant, I called Barry and told him to pump up his promos and go as far and wide as possible.

I found Jane sitting in our living room, peeling carrots and studying a history textbook. Baba was supervising the kitchen while Mama ran the entire floor like a benevolent general. She likes to make recommendations based on customers' tastes and interests, not on what has to be sold. She and Baba fight about that, but her customers walk out happy.

There were several tables of customers I'd never seen before. They all gave an eager puppy-dog stare as I walked in.

"Did Mama put something new in the egg rolls? They're selling fast," Jane said, flipping a page of her textbook.

I lied and said I'd added more white pepper and sweetened the soya sauce.

"Well, those customers out there ordered several, twice, with mustard. They ate them and then complained that they weren't what they expected."

Crap, walk-ins. I told Mama I'd take care of that table. I wanted those new customers to leave and stick to the instructions. Why didn't they just phone like everyone else? Thinking of Barry, I wondered if all stoners were that spaced out.

Mama said no to me taking over the floor. I had four more takeout deliveries. Two were combos, and two were noodle dishes. All the customers wanted egg rolls— with mustard.

I looked at the addresses. Mama's eyes were on me. "What's going on?"

What was going on? I wanted to say: *How the hell did you miss your loan payments? Why don't you tell me what's going on?*

Instead, I shrugged. "Looks like we're busy."

I whispered to the walk-ins that some extra egg rolls might be available on Ross Street. They agreed to meet me. I took care of them outside a couple of dark apartment buildings.

Customers frequently forget to use the mustard code. It's been a pain in the ass. Stoners are stupid. But I manage.

Chapter 23

The New Big Man in School

There is no path to happiness. Happiness is the path. Chinese food is the fuel.

After two weeks of deliveries, something strange has been happening at school. I'm starting to like it. Not the subjects or class—just being around. When I walk down the hall, students give me room. People I hardly know throw me some skin, smile and say hello. I get asked for the lowdown on stuff I know nothing about.

Andrew and I sat in the basement caf, which always smells of French dressing and bleach. Some days, the caf feels like a bomb shelter filled with squirrelly, bored students. The table beside us had a radio playing Zeppelin while some other classmates argued about who was hotter—Wonder Woman or Princess Leia. Andrew joined in and said it was no contest, that Princess Leia was smart and sexy. I still haven't seen *Star Wars*. The students who disagreed laughed and said to dream on

—Wonder Woman was a stone-cold fox and could kick Leia's princess-y ass.

Andrew asked Baahir what he thought. Typically, he sits at the far end of the table, quietly eating. Everyone paused and looked at him. But he didn't even look up from his thermos, which killed that conversation.

Then Angie Dehaut floated in, scanning the caf, looking bored. Her eyes ignored me, sinking my heart. Who was I kidding, thinking she remembered our conversation from that day at the restaurant when I gave her overpriced cigarettes on the house?

She joined the lineup for food and started chatting with Carlos Benevides, the quarterback of the senior football team. He has shoulders like Sylvester Stallone's. He's never without his posse of meatheads. She and Carlos are inseparable, so I assume they're dating. Why couldn't she go for the lean, wiry Spider-Man look like mine? Maybe with a killer workout routine, I could look like Bruce.

"As if, I'm supremely dedicated to working out," Bruce said as he removed his shirt and tightened his abs. "In a way you could be, someday."

As she and the rest of the meatheads approached, Andrew knocked his knee against mine, grinned, and told me to stop drooling at her.

I tried to act innocent, but he saw right through me.

As he was walking closer, Carlos called a student a fag for eating raw vegetables, which drew taunts and limp wrists from the meatheads.

What jerks. Then he stopped at our table. "You Johnny Wong?"

Angie stood beside him, waving at some friends. It

might've been warm in the caf or maybe it was just me, because I got all sweaty. Either way, I waited for her to remove her jacket and reveal more cottonball-soft skin.

I looked up at Carlos Benevides and felt really small and embarrassed by my size. It was then that I realized I'd skipped my morning shower. I smelled of Chinese food: the heaviness of ginger, garlic, onions, soya, and cabbage, the sickly sweet, tangy sauces whose aromas had worked themselves into the fibres of my clothes and my car. I wanted to go home for a long shower, come back, then have Angie lean in for a smell.

I puffed out my chest and straightened my back. "Uh-huh."

"Come sit with us," he said, more like commanded.

I could feel Andrew's eyes on me. But when you're invited to sit at Angie Dehaut's table, you don't hesitate.

Carlos sat between Angie and me and motioned for me to lean into him.

"I sampled an egg roll with mustard the other day. Best stone ever. I wanna get me some for a party this Friday."

With Carlos Benevides talking to me and the school hottie beside him, I felt exposed but also like royalty.

"Yeah, but ... you have to phone and make an order. Free delivery on orders over three dollars."

"Well, can't you just bring some to school? I love Chinese food, even cold." He winked.

"No." I lowered my voice. "I can't do that."

That silenced the other meatheads and drew a look from Angie. We made eye contact, and I was caught. Then she looked away, releasing me.

"I ... guess ... we could do ..." What was I saying? There was no way I was going to peddle dope in the school, not for anything or anybody. Everybody knows the RCMP targets high schools for easy busts. It's not unusual for students to be suspended or even expelled for drugs. "Sorry, Carlos. I can't. It's policy. Sorry."

"Policy? I'm not returning a clock radio at Consumers Distributing. I want to party."

Angie glanced my way from the corner of her eye and smiled at other friends. I'd blown it. Crap.

"No. I mean, I can get you some, but you have to order like everyone else," I said to Carlos.

He squinted, trying to understand how someone had said no to him. Then he patted me on the back. "That's okay, Red Pagoda, right?"

I nodded.

"I'll be calling. It'll be a big party. You can make your delivery and grab a beer. You might as well have some fun, too, Bruce."

A party invite? I was so excited that I pretended not to hear his slight and nodded. Barry was right about weed opening doors, not only with girls but with the cool kids. Getting your first party invitation from the popular kids is both a badge and a burden. You have to look and act like you belong, even if you don't feel like you do.

Carlos told me he was disappointed that *Kung Fu* had been cancelled. He especially liked Master Po, who fought and taught like a demon, despite being blind.

"That's my man, Keye Luke." Bruce jumped onto the table, wrapped a bandana around his eyes, and did a backflip.

"Shut up," I whispered through clenched teeth.

"The son of a gun got stuck playing Charlie Chan roles for years," Bruce said. "I felt sorry for him, so I had him dub the voice of the evil Mr. Han in my last film."

"Yeah, he was my favourite, too," I told Carlos and Bruce. I glanced around the table, resting my eyes maybe too long on Angie.

Carlos leaned in. "We'll be placing an order for some egg foo young and your special egg rolls." He slapped the table as everyone laughed.

He was as funny as a detention. But they were my new friends, so I kept my smile up, not wanting to rock the boat.

It's not the kind of attention I want. Pretty soon, the whole school's going to know. I'm not sure I'm ready for that. Word about me could get to the wrong people. Yet, these students were going to score from someone else anyway. At least none of these guys have stopped me for a hit, not that I ever carry anything. They respect the ordering system.

I saw Mr. Miller manning the main entrance during dismissal. I picked up my pace and tried to duck behind several other students, but he called me over.

He asked me how I was, and I said I was okay. I knew he was going to talk about the college application.

"Johnny, I see you've made some new friends." He didn't look too happy about it.

"I guess."

"Now is not the time to be distracted. Remember," —he pointed at me—"you have a deadline. There might even be a scholarship."

"Yes, sir, thank you." I spied Carlos and Angie, walking toward Manny's. A strong wind blew, and she held the hem of her dress down. I told Mr. Miller I'd started on the application, which was the truth.

I walked over to Nick's, where Andrew was playing the new Evel Knievel pinball game. The flippers were bouncy, and the ball was impossible to control. He tilted the machine and slammed the glass.

"Piece of shit. What a rip-off."

He reached for the cigarette tucked behind his ear. I played a few games. He was right. The machine was shitty.

I thought of telling Andrew about my new weed venture. I figured he'd be cool about it. But I didn't want him involved if things went bad, and I hoped to be done with this soon.

"So, what's with you hanging with those meatheads?" he asked.

I told him Carlos wanted a deal on a big order for a party he was throwing, which was the truth. I changed the conversation to something that would sidetrack him.

"We still going down to shadow Rush at the studio recording?"

He nodded. "Baahir's coming, too."

"I'll believe that when I see it. Where is he, anyway? Usually, he follows me everywhere. I hardly saw him today."

"He's busy with the band tryouts."

"What, Baahir? Get out of here."

"Yeah, he wants to play the guitar. He wants to be the next Alex Lifeson. The guy has a life, believe it or not. I guess he doesn't need you no more."

After school, Baba was in a mood. "Johnny, where have you been? Delivery orders are piling up. Egg rolls are the new pet rocks. Everybody wants them. I even delivered some on foot to a house on Borden."

"You did what?" Christ, parents can be so stupid.

"I walked over an order of egg rolls. It's only around the corner from us, right? They tried to give me forty dollars for four egg rolls. They said "Egg rolls with mustard" like I was stupid. I said yes, eighty cents was enough, but if they wanted to include a tip, they could. But forty dollars, silly gwai lo. I don't know why they looked so sad."

"Baba ..." I shook my head. "Just leave all deliveries for me. You're the inside man."

Chapter 24

Force Field

I ARRIVED AT Carlos's party with egg rolls and a bag of weed. A full ounce sounded like a killer party. He and his friends grabbed the bag and got down to business. I stood by the doorway until Angie came over wearing heavy jewellery and a strapless pink dress with black butterflies, laced with dozens of giant safety pins around her waist. She looked extra pretty.

"I see you got Carlos and the boys their party favours."

"Yeah, I made an early delivery. But I also got something for you." I handed her a small container of har gow. "I hope you like shrimp."

"For me?"

Yes, because you're a stone-cold fox.

"I love shrimp." She opened the container. "Wow, these look great." She took a small bite and then devoured the rest of the dumpling. "Oh my God, this is heavenly. Did you make these?"

"My mother, actually. They're not on the menu, but they're my favourite. I thought you might like them."

"Thank your mother for me." She licked her lips. "You said no to Carlos the other day. I've never seen anybody do that except his mother."

I shrugged. "Well, I'm not his mommy."

She chuckled. "Definitely, you're not. So what makes you different?"

I'd gotten used to "Where are you from?" and "What are you?" But I don't think anybody had asked me what makes me different before. I took deep breaths to control my adrenaline and tried to relax my body like Bruce always did before a takedown. I talked a bit about what books I was reading, and then Carlos walked into the kitchen and poured two rum and Cokes.

"What you got there?" He nodded at the container of har gow.

"Nothing you'd like. Johnny brought these. Shrimp."

Carlos's face scrunched, and then he eyeballed me. For an instant, I thought he would pound me for talking to his girl and bringing her something. Instead, he went to check out some hollering in the next room.

"Does Carlos intimidate you?" Angie said.

It's not like I was going to tell her I had a thing for her, and that Carlos seeing the Chinese delivery boy hitting on his girl was probably cause for him smacking me. "Well, you guys are going out, right? Some guys—"

"We're just friends."

"But you look like a couple."

"That's because we trust and respect one another," she said as she bit into another har gow, "as friends."

I had to think about that. "But friends do not—you know—do it with one another. Who ever heard of that?"

"Why do people assume when a guy and a girl hang, they're automatically doing it? Besides, even if we did, so what? It's nobody's business. Don't you have friends who are girls?"

I lied and said yes.

"Don't you worry about their safety?"

I thought about Jane. Although I can't stand her most of the time, I wouldn't let anything happen to her. "Yes," I said.

We could hear Carlos talking about some quarterback.

"Carlos lives and breathes the NFL," Angie said. "Every second, even when he's high, he trains, talks, and dreams about getting a college scholarship and then playing pro ball. I don't even think he plays the pool."

"The what?"

"It's so vulgar I don't even like to say it. The cherry pool. Boys bet on who's going to pop whose cherry."

I must have looked like I'd eaten a bad shrimp.

She laughed. "You really don't know? At one point, I suddenly started getting so much attention from boys. They bet on who would jump me first. Thankfully, big brother Carlos stepped in and put a stop to that. *Not* like that."

I shook my head in disgust. At those boys, but also because Carlos got to play the hero. On the other hand, that meant she was still a virgin, like me. I liked having that in common.

She sighed. "There are like a million guys in this school and hardly any girls. I mean, did you ever notice that girls don't use the tunnel or the far stairways in the main building? Or why girls never go to the washrooms alone?"

I had never given it any thought. "So?"

"There's a reason for that."

I looked away. It was true. I'd seen and heard what some guys had done in the name of boys being boys and raging hormones. It was shameful.

"Don't feel bad, Johnny. Those guys are jerks. I don't think you're one of them."

But I am one of them. When stuff like that happens at school, I just ignore it, thinking it's none of my business. It reminds me of all the times people have mocked me by pulling back the corners of their eyes, the "chinky chow mein" comments, and the ridiculous fake accents. People laugh along and do nothing, just as I've done nothing while the Angies got groped and attacked. I wish I could've done like Bruce and made it my business.

I wanted to apologize to her, but I had no words. How could I ever be a writer if I couldn't even say a good sorry? I kept my head down and took a deep breath.

"Are you okay, Johnny?" Angie said.

"I'm sorry guys are such jerks. But I get it now. Carlos covers your back."

"That's right." She patted my arm, sending thunderbolts of warmth up my nerves. "I have a mother to look after, I work, and I have teachers from hell. I don't have the time or the energy to watch my back with every step I take in school. Having Carlos as a friend gives me a force field nobody messes with."

She had a point. My life would be much different if I had a force field. Still, I resent Carlos.

So why not date someone like me at the same time?

We moved on to other things and gossiped about who was at the party and who would match up.

I built up some nerve. "How about me? Who'd be a match for me?"

She scanned the room. "I don't know you well enough. But I think you need to be with someone interesting, smart, and who appreciates good food."

Like you?

"Food, right!" I'd actually forgotten. "I have a carload of food to deliver," I said, and made for the door.

I haven't been to many parties, even after three whole years of high school. I walked away reluctantly. I realized Angie and I come from separate sides of the galaxy. Between us are asteroid belts, solar radiation, and extreme heat. I just have to find the right coordinates, because I figure I now have a chance with Angie Dehaut.

Chapter 25

The Egg Roll Factory

SOMETHING UNEXPECTED HAS happened: business has picked up, not just for weed. Even the weed orders have started to include full meals. Some ask for special orders off the menu, the more authentic dishes. Now we're giving extra hours to our part-time staff.

We've become so busy that Mama has little energy left to go out and play mahjong. The only time she did, she came home happy. I guess she won.

I was glad it was Monday and the restaurant was closed. I needed a day off after a month of Barry and special deliveries. We all needed it. It's been years since we did anything together like a normal family. I remember picnicking at Centre Island, catching the dragon dance, and loving the firecrackers every New Year's in Chinatown. But those were never real vacations. We occasionally go out for dinner, but when we do, everyone is quiet. We eat and run in case somebody starts a conversation.

We don't have much of a life outside of the restaurant, not even on days off. Mama and Baba barbeque pork, find chicken deals, top up condiment bottles, chop veggies for the week, and clean.

That Monday, I went straight to our apartment after school.

In my bedroom, I did some shadowboxing and a few low kicks while Bruce, in spandex shorts and boxing gloves, rope-a-doped and rapidly punched.

I was doing a pretty good job, but Bruce refused to accept imperfection. He stopped me. "You are too rigid. Relax, bend, and shapeshift to respond to whatever comes at you mentally and physically."

I told him to calm down.

"I do this by working hard," he said.

Bruce trained and worked day and night. I wondered about his kids. I've seen the footage of his funeral in Hong Kong, where his kids looked so stunned. "Maybe *you* should have relaxed more. I'm sure Brandon would've loved more daddy time."

"Don't talk about my kids, okay?"

The happiest moments of my life were just hanging with Baba. "Trust me, every boy wants more of his father. That's just a given. Even Shannon, I bet, wanted more daddy time."

"I said, don't talk about my kids."

"Now look at who's suddenly forgotten to bend and go with things," I said.

"Shut up." Bruce pointed at me and scowled. "I'm warning you."

"Okay, okay. It's just that when my dad left, I was all busted up." I knew Bruce's father died when Bruce was just a bit older than me, and that his dad never got a chance to see Bruce at his pinnacle. Bruce had likely never filled the hole left behind by his dad, the same one I have.

He stopped moving, and I froze, as the look on his face was so not him. I couldn't tell if it was panic or desperation. You'd think Linda had just left him, which, of course, she never did. You'll never find Bruce sad or melancholy in the movies. Even when he didn't win, he didn't lose.

Whatever it was, we're not supposed to go there.

I returned to my English essay on *The Outsiders*. S.E. Hinton was eighteen years old when it was published. I like complicated stories where guys do bad stuff even though they mean well. I mean, if a teenager can write this, who's to say I can't?

My stomach kicked with hunger and I hadn't eaten since lunch, so I stepped into the restaurant through the back and into the kitchen. Once in a while, I want some Wonder Bread. No rice, ginger, soy, garlic, or green onions. Just plain white toast slathered with butter. A couple of egg rolls were on the counter when I got downstairs. I hadn't had one in a while, and though my mind was on toast, the rolls were still hot, almost like Mama knew I would be coming. I bit into one. It was hot! So hot I had to roll it around in my mouth. After a few bites, I peeled back the fried wrapper and looked inside. It really was good. It might even explain some of the extra egg roll sales without mustard.

I heard clanging and banging coming from the restaurant's dining room. The warm glow of golden hour and a single overhead light shone on our "living room" where Mama sat with her back to me. In front of her was a bowl of egg roll filling and wrappers. Beside that was the beat-up Tele-Tone portable record player Baba had dug out of someone's garbage, thinking it was a tiny suitcase. She'd gotten it going, had cued the needle on the record player, and had put on one of her Chinese operas—all gongs, cymbals, and fiddle. It was pure torture—worse than the junior band tryouts.

Mama had tried to explain Chinese opera to me at various times in my life, but you might as well have made me eat cold, lumpy porridge. It wasn't until she told me that Bruce's father was a famous classically trained opera singer and that his training included weapons, acrobatics, and kung fu that I'd agreed to listen to her albums with her.

She'd explained that the music from the orchestra of eight to ten players is in synch with the stage actors, all of whom wear dazzling robes that would make a peacock look like a wet crow. Pointing to her colourful album covers, she'd drilled the characters into me. There's the Laosheng, the gentle, cultivated warrior or official with a fake long beard. There's Wusheng, whom I remember because he always gets to swing swords and spears and jump around like a maniac. There are a few more, but the only other one I remember is Qingyi, the most important character, always dressed in yellow and usually the strict mama who's serious and dignified.

Mama told me when she was a girl, she fell in love with the Qingyi character and wanted to play her someday. But her mother laughed at her and said women were banned from performing. Looking closely at Qingyi at the next opera, Mama realized a man was playing her.

Mama has said the key to understanding who's who is to recognize the patterns in the face masks. Each actor has unique techniques and interpretations, and each character has a set face type between which audiences can distinguish. They all just looked hideously over-made and exaggerated to me.

I watched Mama fill many of the square egg roll wrappers before taking a break to get into the music. She bent her head slightly and brought her hand in front of her eyes to symbolize weeping. As the opera continued, her singing drowned out the recording. I'd heard the ballad, "A Young Girl's Dream," many times before. It occasionally pops into my head like a coarse earworm. She raised her hands high with her palms down, then jerked her head and grimaced, flicking her sleeves outward. I knew that meant happiness. All this was in step with the music.

She returned to the egg rolls and quickly formed a pile but continued to sing along. Even with her face tensed up, she sounded, and I never thought I'd say this, emotional yet also relaxed, something I hadn't seen in a while.

When she first explained the Chinese opera to me, she'd wanted me to understand what was happening: how the shrieking sounds punctuate the movements and support the singing, facial expressions, and weird gestures. The clanging, the squealing, the jerkiness, the hand motions—each needing the other—were crude and annoying. But Mama looked like a pro, singing and moving along. The lyrics could have been about bean sprouts for all I know, but the song seemed to make her happy.

She stopped midmovement and turned her head toward me.

"Gwo lai." She called me over and said to bring the other hot egg roll.

She slid the plate of square wrappers and the filling bowl between us, then kicked a chair out for me.

The song soon ended and an awkward silence followed as I started filling and rolling.

"Too much filling," she said.

"I know what I'm doing." At least, I thought so—until I saw how she did three perfectly tight, chubby cigar rolls out of my two. Mine were perfect if you didn't compare them with how even and aligned every fold of hers was. She lit a cigarette with her left hand and continued rolling with her right.

"When I was your age, I thought I knew what I was doing. I had a dream. I was going to be an opera star. Then I came to Canada, and things happened. It doesn't matter. A long time ago."

I just about fell out of my seat. That was as revealing as she ever got.

"These are magic egg rolls." The corner of her mouth gripped her cigarette as she exhaled.

I nodded without looking up. "Ho sik wa." They were delicious. "Did you change the recipe?"

She listed the usual ingredients.

"They're the best," I said. "They were already good, your old recipe, I mean. But the addition of tiny bits of homemade diced barbeque pork and oyster mushroom are flavour bombs no one else is doing."

She gave me a sharp look and said she changed the recipe months ago. "Same egg roll. Why is it so popular all of a sudden?"

She had this tone where I didn't know whether it was a statement or an accusation, and I was left off-balance, unsure of what to say.

"And on days you work. Funny."

I sped up, hoping to get through this batch. "I work most days, Mama."

"And mustard. Funny. Very funny." She switched to Toisanese, which I always struggled to keep up with. "What do you have to say?"

"They've been discovered. Maybe we should sell nothing but these and call ourselves the Egg Roll Factory?" I laughed to divert the conversation. "We could have other flavours and fillings. We could target parties and business meetings, create new combos with salads for all those people on diet pills."

I had failed to distract her.

The needle on the record player skipped, repeating crackles and hisses. She ignored it. I overstuffed a roll and threw it upside down into the pile, hoping she wouldn't notice.

"People phone and hang up all the time now. Sometimes, they come in for an egg roll, look around, and leave mad. They don't even try the food. They are just mad. Not funny."

I tore a wrapper accidentally and attempted to patch it up, but it looked awful. I know she noticed.

"Business is good, Johnny. But I worry—"

"Worry about what? Making money? Since when is that a problem?"

"I worry you are getting yourself into something. Am I wrong?"

My last two rolls were all uneven and sloppy. "I'm fine, the restaurant's fine, school's fine."

The skipping on the record player was driving me crazy.

"This restaurant is not everything," she said.

I stopped rolling. "It's not? Because it's not paying off your debt to Auntie?" That came out like a killer mahjong hand I'd revealed prematurely because I'd gotten impatient and foolish.

She stopped rolling. "That is none of your business. You do not understand. Do not—"

"What don't I understand? What?"

"There are things we must do in a family."

That's because you're a loser, and I'm saving your ass. I studied her face and waited for a sign, a hint of what was beneath. Interpreting her silence as weakness, I gambled. "You know, if you made more of an effort with Auntie, she might get off your case about paying her back."

She gave me this Medusa glare like she was going to slap me, something she hadn't done since forever. She'd never really had to. That look turned me into a seven-year-old again. My body recoiled, and my fists balled.

I relaxed once I remembered something my English teacher from last year, Mrs. Laskin, said about Medusa being misunderstood. She's not a monster but an enraged, fearsome protector of women's secrets. Maybe she wasn't trying to scare me—maybe she was hiding behind that look.

She glanced around to make sure no one else was within earshot. We basically never talked about the past. Seeing that the coast was clear, she gave me the stock parent answer—that things were more complicated. She turned the record over and dropped the needle a little too hard. Screeching opera filled the restaurant.

"More complicated than what?" I asked.

"My business with your aunt is not your concern."

I wanted to say that bailing this family out has always been my business. I could handle that complication.

"Your aunt and I are a lot alike. We've both had to live by rules made by other people."

I wanted to ask what she meant. Who were those "other people"—the gwai lo?

We finished wrapping the remaining egg rolls, sitting in our awkward silence. I slid my chair out and went to the kitchen to clean up. Before going upstairs, I glanced back at her. She was unwrapping some of my egg rolls, redoing my work. Making perfect the imperfections I'd created.

Chapter 26

The Makeup Artist

AFTER LEAVING MAMA to finish the egg rolls, I decided to get some new threads. Andrew had been wanting to go to the new Eaton Centre, but I decided to go by myself because something weird was going on between us —like he was jealous that I was hanging out with Carlos and Angie. I took the College streetcar to Yonge Street and walked down.

Yonge Street is like an anthill of the biggest and loudest cars, the biggest and brightest neon signs, and half the city, who all crave excitement. I bet the street's blast of light is visible from outer space. Right away, a homeless man asked me for money. Storefronts were cranking out music while sidewalk buskers jostled for attention.

I walked on and was offered hash, salvation through God, shoes, electronics, army surplus gear, movie tickets, books, sex toys, and more hash. Then, a punk rocker with a purple mohawk handed me a coupon for a "special massage with extras." I weaved my way down the street, past body-rub parlours, topless bars, X-rated adult bookstores and theatres, and the clacks and dings and bells of arcades. Ignoring them was impossible.

I fantasize about Angie all the time, but it's never like the way women are depicted on these buildings, with boobs popping out of their halter tops, and no way do I imagine her on all fours with a leash around her neck.

People say how dangerous and scuzzy that area is. I never thought of it when I was a kid roaming the streets, which, when I think about it, was stupid.

I went into Coles bookstore and browsed through the bestseller list, fantasizing about my name appearing beside J.R.R. Tolkien and Leon Uris. On my way out, I picked up a pocket thesaurus. I jumped into a head shop to look at a Bruce Lee poster special: Buy any one item, get the second half off. There were posters of all his movies: Bruce in fight poses, Bruce sweating, Bruce's steel abs and bloody scratches, Bruce's nunchucks, Bruce in a midair kick. Also, a serious one of his face in black and white with a saying: "Do not pray for an easy life, pray for the strength to endure a difficult one." I bought that one and another that said: "Notice that the stiffest tree is most easily cracked, while the bamboo or willow survives by bending with the wind."

"Good choices. Those are two of my favourites," Bruce said as he did side kicks with his shirt off. "Now, let's go check out the ladies at the mall."

Across the street was the Eaton Centre—a big bright futuristic glass shopping cathedral with escalators climbing to the sky and shoppers everywhere. I wandered through some of the hundreds of stores and then the food court, where loads of other teenagers and hot girls were hanging out. No wonder Andrew wanted to come down. I looked at the menus at the Chinese takeout restaurants. They all serve the same dishes as us, except for our special egg rolls.

I scored a pair of Kodiaks, Wranglers, and a plaid flannel shirt, but then I got lost looking for the exit to Dundas Street. In the makeup section, I stopped. There was Jane by herself, looking shy and cute with her mouth open and head slightly tilted to one side. Baba still falls for that. She was supposed to be at her piano lessons.

A couple of years ago, Mama caught her playing with her makeup. I thought Mama was going to freak out. Instead, she gently cleaned it off Jane's face. Mama said we all wear makeup and masks. It is easier to hide who we are and what we feel. She said face-masking is important to Chinese opera and that there are twenty-six types of eyebrows, with names like *the butterfly*, *the bat*, and *the duck*. Mama painted one style on Jane, who shone and wanted to see the other eyebrows. Mama turned it into a game, making us guess each shape's name. It was a rare moment of fun with Mama. That was until Baba came in. Once he saw Jane all made up, he accused Mama of trying to make her look like a tramp. Mama accused him of knowing all about tramps. He fired back that he wasn't going to let his daughter become a lowlife bum like Mama. They went at it for a while. Eventually, Jane and I slithered away, leaving them to scorch the earth.

A baby wailed in the mall. Jane slipped the eyeliner up her sleeve, then slowly looked around to see if anyone saw it. Her gaze stopped at me.

She smiled, called out my name, and walked toward me like nothing had happened.

I grabbed her by the arm. "What the hell do you think you're doing? Put that back."

"Put what back, dai goh?"

Calling me *big brother* like that was a total mock.

"I saw what you did. What are you doing here anyway? You're supposed to be at piano."

"Mr. Lim is an evil taskmaster who picks his nose while I play. I called in sick. I wanted a snot-free day."

I shook my head. "Does Baba know?"

"He knows I'm the perfect daughter, and that you are the number-one son in a soon-to-be national chain of Red Pagodas from Vancouver to Saint John."

Damn. "Look, put it back, let's just go home."

"I have a better idea. I'd like the new Andy Gibb on vinyl, but I'll settle for the album on cassette. We'd make a wonderfully cute and innocent-looking couple. Let's go to Sam's. You can cover my back."

"What are you, crazy? That's stealing."

"Yeah, that's so wrong. We could sell dope instead, maybe some egg rolls with mustard?"

I wish I could have done a fake smile like her. After a long silence, I was so psyched out, all I could say back was that she was talking jive.

"Who's jive-talking? Barry Arble suddenly comes in like a white knight. We sell lots of egg rolls, and they all ask for it with mustard—sounds suspicious. Then business picks up, Mama and Baba are too blinded by the money rolling in, and I'm getting the new Andy Gibb album because ... *he just wants to be my everything.*" She sang that last little bit to rub it in.

"Jesus Christ. How did you know?"

"Johnny, we get more callers hanging up than actual orders. And strangely, usually from four to six, when you're on, our delivery orders are crazy. Coincidence, maybe?"

"A total coincidence," I said.

"Well, we also have two phones on the same line. I've heard them ask if it's Colombian Gold or sinsemilla. Those are your smarter customers. The losers come in asking for egg rolls and mustard. Once they get their egg rolls and nothing else, they walk out mad. How long before you get busted, the whole restaurant is shut down, and we go to jail?"

"You listened in on my calls?"

A saleswoman came over. "Can I help you with anything?"

I wanted Jane to give the eyeliner back, but I knew she'd make a scene. "We're fine, miss, thank you. Which way is Dundas Street?"

She pointed to the exit.

Once we were out on the corner of Yonge and Dundas, I asked Jane why.

Her face lost its innocent look. "When you've played with fire, you don't need water."

That was the first time I've heard her mention the big fire she started years ago.

She shrugged. "This is the way it is. Besides, can you imagine how crazy things will be once they find out? I'll enjoy the quiet and have fun before all hell breaks loose."

My heart sank a bit. "No. I've taken precautions. You know nothing. You've seen nothing. I don't keep anything inside."

"What a smarty pants, making sure Mama doesn't mistake it for oregano." She had done a great job convincing Baba she was the perfect daughter. No wonder she was so cocky. She was almost untouchable. "You coming?" She pointed at the enormous sign, two neon spinning vinyl discs, unmistakably Sam the Record Man.

"No, stop."

She darted up Yonge Street, crossing on a red light. She paused before the Rio Theatre, which advertised three Dirty Harry movies on the marquee. A red Cadillac convertible stopped and honked. Jane flashed a look of curiosity and turned toward it.

I tore across Dundas, cutting in front of a motorist, who gave me the finger. Then I ran up Yonge. The driver of the Caddy lowered the passenger-side window and then leaned across to say something to Jane, who smiled and looked into the car as the driver opened the door. I shot across the street and pushed her along as a police car pulled up behind the Caddy. The driver slammed his door and sped off.

I could barely catch my breath. "What are you, stupid?"

She nodded. "It runs in the family, doesn't it?" She continued toward the spinning neon sign and went into the record store. I stood guard outside, asking Bruce for the strength to endure whatever she was up to.

Chapter 27

Let the Good Times Roll

BABA WAS IN a good mood. Mama's been staying home recently, sleeping at decent hours, and hasn't missed a shift in a while. Business is still picking up. Mama bought paper lanterns and Halloween decorations and has hung them around the restaurant. What's really weird is that Mama and Baba smiled and giggled as they did it, like they were having fun and getting along. Missing were the usual cutthroat silence and strained tension.

They talked about gradual updates to the restaurant, like repainting, playing music in the background, replacing all our chipped dishes, and someday laying a new floor.

Baba was able to replace the ventilation and suggested we hire a driver. When I said I'd gotten used to driving and didn't mind, Mama's eyes bore into me.

I knew the money was coming in from stoners ordering more food. They'd become repeat customers. Sometimes, they skipped the weed and only ordered dinner.

I hadn't expected this increase in business or the new vibe between my parents, and I'm not entirely sure how to feel about it. It all makes me wonder how long the good times can last.

Chapter 28

The Art of Flirting

THE NEXT DAY at school, during period change, Trevor Heywood pulled the corners of his eyes back to tease me. Before I could say or do anything, Pasquale and Domenic pinned him to the wall, smacking his head like a pinball.

Pasquale threatened Trevor that if he pulled that stuff again, his head would be flattened like a pizza pie. Domenic called him a stupid mangiacake before Trevor crumpled to the ground.

Domenic waved me over. "You keep up the killer smoke, and you won't have to worry about him anymore." He said they'd see me later in the caf or at Manny's after school.

Barry had said weed opened doors to girls but never mentioned the football team.

Bruce leaned on a locker and smirked. "Your boys got carried away. I guess you won't be needing me anymore?"

"Trevor's a jerk, he deserved it. You laid out a thousand guys like that."

"And you know why? It is because I could not walk away. Martial arts are an art form. It is an unrestricted athletic expression of an individual soul. What do you call that?" He pointed at Trevor, still on the ground, cradling his head.

"Piss off, Bruce. Sometimes, you sound so high and mighty, like a big show-off. It's easy for you to run your mouth and tell me to 'stop thinking, show emotions, and do.' Well, I'm doing stuff. And if Trevor gets in my way, what's wrong with letting someone else do the doing?"

"You will never win over the Trevors that way," Bruce said.

"Who cares?" I looked around to make sure no one was listening. Nobody cared. Bruce vanished, and I rushed to geography, where some classmates winked and thanked me for the egg rolls.

It was lab day. It used to be that nobody wanted to be in a group with me except for Andrew and Baahir. But Mario and Jose waved me over. I'd seen them stoned out of their minds at Carlos's party, having a great time. Andrew looked hurt, like he'd been kicked in the gut. Baahir briefly made eye contact with me, then looked away as though I'd disappointed him.

I shrugged. It was no big deal. Be like that, I thought.

Students burst out of the school at lunch, ready to flood the arcades and fast-food joints surrounding CTS. I saw Angie leaving the art building. She turned onto the service road, which separated the track and field from the main building, no doubt heading for Manny's.

Bruce materialized, straightened up his UW jacket and sunglasses, and smiled. "Ask her out, Johnny."

"Piss off," I whispered. "When I'm ready."

He grinned. "Don't think, do."

"I'm not you," I said. There is no way I could score without Bruce's coolness and confidence.

"Ask her out."

I was about to tell Bruce to shut up when Angie surprised me by calling me over.

We exchanged hellos and walked along. After an uncomfortable silence, I tried to be really impressive and told her about my application for a West Connecticut scholarship.

"Really?" She hugged me, which was almost as good as a big wet kiss. "That's far out. I just know you're going to get it." She told me about her plans to attend the Ontario College of Art, and then she stopped walking and pulled back the protective sheet to reveal a painting she was working on. A quick gust of wind almost took the painting out of her grasp. When she recovered, she righted the painting to reveal a nude woman with big arms and thighs, breasts exposed, and arms covering her face like she was shy but not scared.

"That's Art Deco?" In my drafting class, we'd discussed design and how styles like Art Deco influence art, architecture, and even furniture. I think I was the only one who didn't fall asleep.

"I'm impressed, Johnny." She smiled. "I'll give you ten bonus points if you can tell me who influenced this." Angie pointed to her nude.

I wished we could just talk about books. That would've been easier. I must have looked like I was drowning. So, I tried to be funny instead of smart. "I don't know—Pablo Pistachio? Vincent Price?"

She chuckled. "You get five points for trying. It's Tamara de Lempicka. I'm copying her *Das Modell*."

Her good humour loosened me up. "What do you like about her?"

"I like how she uses bold, sensual, sometimes lesbian women with swooping curves and tight muscles. She had such assurance in her work. I especially like that she was a very confident woman at a time when women were supposed to shut up and cook. She put up with a lot of crap and did her own thing and rebelled against tradition."

"You mean she was a feminist?"

"Yeah, exactly, de Lempicka didn't put up with other people's garbage. You're pretty smart, aren't you?"

I shrugged.

"I mean, I had heard you wrote something in the *Blow* last year about police brutality. No wonder you're going to West Connecticut. That sure makes you different."

I pretended to be shy about this, but damned if I wasn't proud to impress her.

"You're a man of many faces. From a crusader against excessive police force to delivering weed."

"It's a temp job—dealing, I mean. I have standards. I don't deal at school, definitely not with children, and nothing more than weed."

She nodded in approval.

"It's not something I want to do for much longer. I'm just trying to help my family out."

"I get that. Because why would you want to do this when you're going to an American college?"

I changed the subject and studied her painting. "Not quite a Princess Leia, but strong, right?"

"I must be the last person on the planet who hasn't seen *Star Wars*."

My eyes lit up. "You and me both."

"Really? I don't see what the big deal is. But I should probably see what everybody's talking about."

"Yeah, me too," I said.

I let that sink in.

Bruce did some side bends and then stopped. "What are you waiting for? Ask her out." He returned to his side bends.

Two students were whipping a football back and forth nearby. I liked how they noticed me walking with Angie.

I took my shot. "You want to see it? I mean, like friends."

Bruce smacked me in the head. "Why did you say *like friends*? Do you want to do a group project or kiss her?"

Much to my relief and joy, she said yes. We arranged to meet outside the Uptown Theatre at Yonge and Bloor on Tuesday after school. In a state of disbelief, I watched her walk away. Not wanting to blow my chance, I thought of running to the library to read about this Lempicka artist.

Bruce patted me on the back. "Way to go."

"You think she likes me?"

He shrugged. "Enough to go to the movies. You know what you have to do now, don't you?"

"Train?"

He did a front flip onto the track and waved me on before tearing it down. I followed suit, yelled, and ran a victory lap along the asphalt track, imagining myself with my shirt off, muscles on muscles like Bruce.

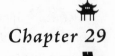

Chapter 29

Searching for the Golden Boy

BARRY HAS BEEN coming around most nights, either early in the evening or when we're closing. He'll pop in and out, chatting up Jane and my parents and just getting in the way.

"Shouldn't you be handing out flyers and samples or whatever a marketing-and-promotions specialist does?"

Like a little boy on a merry-go-round, he spun around on one of our squeaky counter stools and told me, "I'm pacing myself. I don't want to spread myself too thin. Hey, you need to oil these stools, man. Get to work, chop, chop."

We're in business, serious business, and him acting like a child and pissing me off is really starting to bug me. Am I overly sensitive? How much more of this can I take?

I told him to buzz off. He left for a beer across the street but returned to divide the evening's take of $330. My share, he informed me, would be $110, not including tips, which I did well on because I was always polite when they opened the door. With every customer, I made myself smile like it was someone special—like Angie—welcoming me in.

In a month, we had sold over a pound. I had paid Auntie two more instalment payments and now had another eight hundred dollars ready to drop off. Once Auntie's paid off, I can just walk away from the Barry partnership. But if I stay on, I might be able to afford college, too.

Barry restocked the car with a pound divided into 450 dime bags, each a bit less than a gram. He said it had taken him days to clean out, weigh, and bag the dope.

"That's a lot," I said, shaking my head.

"This is safer than me carrying a small stash to meet you every night. Besides, you have a good hiding spot in the garage. We'll sell out before we know it, you'll see."

He was right. Orders were picking up, and word was getting around that the Red Pagoda sold primo stuff. What I really needed was another driver or someone to work the street. But I wasn't going to leave that in the car, so I hid most of it in the garage rafter, taking out only what I needed for the evening.

I told him I was headed to the Association. I had to explain that it was a bit of a club, and that our family often did business with them. Any more than that, I knew he'd zone out. He agreed to ride shotgun. But once he saw the building, he insisted on waiting in the car around the corner. He slid over to the driver's seat and kept the car running, even though the engine idled rough.

"This is such a shitbox car, Johnny. Time to get a new ride."

He was right, but a new car isn't something we can afford yet.

One of Auntie's boys, Stanley, guarded the door. He let me in. I peeked into the main room, where a few games were on the go while other people drank tea and read Chinese dailies. I made my way upstairs into the high rollers' room. They were between games. I asked where Leo and his mother were. I was told they were in the basement storage room and I needed to wait.

I had eight hundred dollars bundled in my Kodiaks. I wasn't going back. I knew she'd want this money, so I walked downstairs and found the storage-room door ajar.

Auntie was twisting Leo's ear. It looked painful.

"What do you mean you do not know?" She twisted harder until his ear was purple, and he cried out and pulled back. She said, "Mo yung doi."

Getting called a useless and worthless wretch is about the worst thing a Chinese mother can say to their kid. Not having any value, worth, or benefit to the family is like being a zero, or even worse, a minus.

"You find whoever he is. You bring the Golden Boy who stole from us to me. He's probably not working alone. Is that too much to ask?" She released him, then noticed me. "Johnny, what are you doing here? Leo and I were just having a family discussion."

I wondered who'd stolen what as I half bowed and explained why I was there. I took my boot off and handed her the roll of bills. She didn't care that the money was sweaty. She counted bills like a bank clerk, then used the stack to slap Leo across the cheek.

"This is how a son behaves." She pointed at me and then looked at her son. "This is how a son looks after his mama. Why are you so useless and not like Johnny?"

"Auntie, Leo has always been respectful and full of praise when speaking about you."

"Pff." She waved me off, but then stared at me. "How are you getting money like this?"

I blinked. "Work. Business is good. I appreciate you keeping your end of the bargain. In another couple months, we should be clear." Not soon enough. I'd paid nine hundred dollars in interest already.

"Business must be good. I should come up and pay a visit, see for myself, say hello to your mama."

"Sure, we'd like that. Remember, we understand that this repayment is not for her to know."

She waved me off again. "Yes, yes. She got an extension because I am kind-hearted and caring." She broke into a rare smile. "You look after things, I like that. That is why you should work for me instead of delivering garbage food."

I didn't like her saying that about our restaurant. My parents work hard. They never say they enjoy the long hours, but it matters to them and to us. We all chip in. It's not food we eat, but the gwai lo love it. It's not garbage.

"My duty is to my parents, Auntie. Isn't that what you have been saying?"

She smirked at Leo. "Did you hear that?"

He left without a word.

"You see the attitude I get, Johnny?"

When I returned to the car, Barry was all freaked out. "I thought you got robbed or something."

I had to tell him to take a chill pill, that I had everything under control like I always did.

"Forget about it. Let's go out and celebrate," he said.

"Celebrate? Sure, where?"

"A titty bar." His blue eyes lit up like a Christmas tree.

Chapter 30

The Zanzibar

BARRY LAUGHED WHEN I told him I couldn't go to the titty bar because it was a school night. It did sound dorky.

"Come on, one drink. I'm buying. What do you care about school? It'll make a man out of you."

He dragged me to the Zanzibar, one of many strip joints on Yonge Street. Since I'd started hanging with Carlos, I'd heard some kids at our school had snuck in with fake ID. Apparently, the Hells Angels ran it and made the dancers go nude even though it was against the law.

"You've been in?" I asked.

He looked at me like I'd never seen snow. Anybody who's ever set foot on Yonge Street knows of the Zanzibar or the Brass Rail, two of the biggest strip joints. Their storefront signs advertise topless girls all day, along with lunch specials.

The whole sex strip's been getting cleaned up after the murder of that immigrant shoeshine boy. But unlike the brothels and peep shows that have opened in the last few years, the Zanzibar has been here forever, and shutting it down would be like draining an ocean.

"I'm not sure I can get in. I don't have ID."

"Johnny Boy, you look and act like an old man already. Just drop that kung fu stare and act like you belong," Barry said as we approached the entrance.

Three Hulks guarded the door, one with tattoos on his bare arms and neck. They turned away a couple of guys trying to get in. But Barry stepped right up, shook hands with each of the bouncers, and they all joked like old friends.

"My mother in?" Barry asked.

The bouncers shook their heads.

"She might be at the new Den 4 Men in Scarborough. I heard they got some dumb Japanese jukebox that plays music while customers sing into a mic."

The Hulks laughed and gave me a look like I would know something about it. I remembered what Barry said and looked them in the eye, one by one, adding Bruce's best stoic, kung fu master stare. I hated doing that. It's that feeling of being dipped in old fry grease. But I got over it fast once one of them waved us in.

"How do you know those guys?"

"I used to hang around here when my mother worked here."

I'd forgotten she was a stripper. "You'd watch your mother strip?"

"No, you idiot. There was a TV and bar in the basement, and I got all the fries and Coke I wanted. The best part is that the dancers changed and hung out down there. Everybody loved me. I'm a charmer."

We stepped inside to the thundering sounds of "Da Ya Think I'm Sexy?" by Rod Stewart.

A thick wall of smoke stung my eyes and forced them shut. I stopped. I blinked several times, then saw Barry snaking his way past dozens of small round tables spread out on a huge floor. Black walls and dark wood panelling decorated the large room. A long bar with stools was between the stage and the front door.

"What would you do if your mother was working now?" I yelled into his ear.

"I'd say hello, of course. What would you do?"

I couldn't imagine how messed up it would be to see Mama dancing naked—no wonder Barry got bounced around foster homes.

The thick clouds of cigarette smoke and the smell of stale sweat and beer made me want to gag. I felt awkward and not sure I wanted to stay. Barry waved at staff as he grabbed two seats in front of the stage. A waitress dressed as a Dallas Cowboys cheerleader came over in white high-cut shorts, white knee-high boots, and a blue halter top. She had long dark wavy hair like Angie. Her large boobs spilled out of her halter top.

Barry chatted her up before she walked away.

"What a fox. Don't be so shy." Barry laughed. "I ordered for us."

The waitress returned pretty fast. I was impressed. A part-timer at the Red Pagoda had just quit, and I wondered if she'd be interested in split shifts. But I doubted she and Mama would get along.

She dropped off two rum and Cokes and two tequilas, charging us almost ten dollars.

"I thought you said one drink?" I yelled.

Barry ignored me and paid. He asked her to exchange a twenty-dollar bill for twenty singles, giving her one as a tip.

Barry sang along to the music and said we were celebrating. He held his glass up. I did the same.

"What are we celebrating, anyway?"

His eyes followed another waitress. "We're successful businessmen, Johnny Boy, just getting started."

"What do you mean, just getting started?"

"I'm going to get more product."

"What?" I yelled above the music.

"More weed," he hollered. "I'm going to score us more weed."

I looked around to see if anyone was listening, but the music was loud, and no one seemed to be paying attention to us. "Why? Don't we have enough?"

"Johnny, what are you doing with your money?"

I wasn't going to say anything about Auntie. "The Pagoda. It goes back into the restaurant."

He patted me on the back, then raised his glass. "Such a good son you are." He gulped his drink down and waved at our waitress. "Drink up, Johnny Boy. I'm using my money to party and score us another load. We got a good thing going. Yep, I'm exploring what they call them—supply chains? I'm going to set aside some money for a house, maybe one with a granny suite."

"Why?"

"For my mother, of course. But first, I'll buy myself a CB radio and one of those waterbeds." He made wavy motions with his hands and talked into his closed fist. "This here's the Big B, ten-four."

Another load? I don't want to know where and how he plans to get more weed. I'm pretty sure this isn't something I want to do for longer than I have to. Just until my family's clear, then I'm out.

I sipped my rum and Coke and had to admit it tasted alright. Barry led the way downing the shooters. It burned, going down like bits of glass. The waitress came over with two more rum and Cokes. I slurped my first one and handed her the empty glass. I suddenly felt warm. My head got mushy like a shifting beanbag.

The waitress stood there smiling. She said something that sounded like a phone number. Did she want to go out? I smiled back, hoping she hadn't caught me staring at her boobs. I reached into my jacket for a pen.

"Your wallet's in your back pocket. Pay the lady," Barry yelled in my ear, laughing. "And don't forget to tip."

I handed over six dollars and swore at myself for being stupid. The waitress moved on.

The DJ cut the music and came on, saving me from further embarrassment. "Gentlemen, are you readeee?" Theatre lights lit up the empty stage's wall of tinsel.

A few hoots came through.

"I can't heaaar you," the DJ taunted. "Are you ready for our next sizzling sensation?"

A scattering of "woo hoos" and someone yelling "Bring us some honey" made for a weak response.

"Now, gentlemen, our next act can be a bit shy, so you'll have to make some noise for our next dancer— Cleopatra, Queeen of the Desert." The lights shone on a dancer who slow-walked onstage with a rubber boa constrictor wrapped around her.

Barry and I downed another round. He asked every dancer and waitress about his mother, getting the same head shake.

Cleopatra slithered the fake snake between her legs and around her body. I scanned the crowd, who looked like they were sitting in math class, chewing gum, waiting for the bell to ring. Other guys, like Barry, hooted and hollered for her attention with dollar bills. I didn't know what to think or do, so I hunched over and drank.

Barry had ordered two more tequila shooters. They grated my throat. I coughed.

My vision started to blur. Thankfully, Barry had ordered two stubbies also, and I guzzled the soothing cold beer. All of a sudden, I couldn't sit or stand straight. I studied Cleopatra and realized something was dreadfully wrong.

"Hey. Hey," I yelled. Cleopatra ignored me, so I tried to get Barry to understand, but he was smoothing out dollar-bill offerings.

"Desert climate ... not good for boas." I shook my head, but that only made me dizzy. Pretty soon, I was talking to myself and peeling the edges off the bottle's label. "Viper, yes. Cobra, yes. Boa, no. Why doesn't anybody listen to me?" After two more dancers and another round, I told Barry I had to leave.

"Don't be stupid." He waved the waitress over and ordered two more stubbies of Labatt 50.

My eyes lingered on her as she walked down from the stage after her set. Her ocean-blue eyes were similar to Angie's, but Cleopatra looked like an older version. I asked if she also liked de Lempicka's nudies.

She looked confused. I leaned in so she could better hear me, but I stood and stumbled toward her, almost grabbing her to brace a fall. I startled her.

"No touching," she hollered, then moved on.

"Johnny, Johnny," Barry screamed into my ear. "Let me give you a warning. If you touch one of the girls, those bouncers will kick your head in so fast, you'll wish you were never born."

That made me think of Angie and all the other girls at school who had to avoid parts of our school because of creeps. I yelled an apology to the waitress, but she was already serving another table.

"What are you talking about? I would never do that."

"Just saying. You're pretty wasted."

I thought about what Barry had said about expanding supply chains. It could work. We had a good thing going. I could hold everybody together and keep the restaurant open. The hell with college, with writing. Who needs that spoiled, pampered, elitist crap? All I wanted was moneeey.

Suddenly, the room started spinning, and I couldn't hold my pee in any longer. I tried to be cool but almost fell as I got off the chair.

"Where are you going?" Barry laughed.

"I gotta piss. Now." The lights blurred together, and I couldn't see a washroom. Barry grabbed my arm as I stumbled, and the room spun faster.

Barry told me to hang on. "Not here, not here." He dragged me through a maze of tables and down a set of stairs to the washroom.

"I don't feel good," I mumbled.

Barry kicked in the washroom door and led me to a toilet clogged with bricks of shit. I turned my head and barfed on the floor and my new Kodiaks.

We took the streetcar home, and I sat by the open window, catching the cool evening air. I'd run out of insides to barf out and I was sagging like a rag doll. I could hear Barry, who was still having a good time, chatting with nearby passengers. He leaned over to check on me. I lied and told him I was okay.

"Barry," I mumbled, "you want to save for a house?"

He took his eyes off a girl on the streetcar. "Fuck yeah. Someday, I want to be king of my castle and bounce three kids up and down the beer gut I'm working on. I gotta set my mother up, too."

"Hell no, not you, too," I muttered.

"What?"

I didn't have the energy to laugh and say that I couldn't believe he had a dream. He'd thought of a future. It sounded so square. But he had goals, just like Andrew did.

He punched me in the arm. "Time to lose your Batman utility belt, Johnny Boy. You're a man now."

I didn't feel like one. I just wanted to go home.

Chapter 31

Date Night

I DOUBTED BRUCE ever got nervous before a date.

"Actually, I nearly shit my pants before my first date with Linda. I just never showed any weakness," he said, wearing a pirate shirt, bell-bottoms, and sunglasses. "Besides, you must use that nervous tension. Be one with it. Use it to your advantage."

I wasn't sure how I would do that. I didn't want his voice distracting me, so I blasted Rush's "Closer to the Heart."

All day long, I thought of being with Angie. I was calling it a date even though we'd agreed that, technically, it wasn't. I'd just *had* to go and say "as friends." Still, I wanted it to be perfect. Nothing else mattered. I remembered I was supposed to meet Andrew for a few games at Manny's after school and doubled back.

I was late, and Andrew was pissed. I didn't need that and told him not to be such a crybaby.

"What's up with you, man? It's like you're ignoring us. I bet you forgot about Rush coming up." He sounded hurt. It should've mattered, but to be honest, at that moment, I didn't give a shit, and he could probably tell. My attention wandered as I saw Angie and Carlos driving off in a Monte Carlo. I swear she saw me and smiled.

"Yo ... you're not even listening to me." Andrew snapped me back to attention.

"Christ, how many times are you going to ask me? I said I'd come, didn't I?"

He told me I was uptight and had become a snob.

I said "Whatever" and left. What a drama queen.

I ironed my plaid shirt and jeans, washed my hair, and rubbed in some Brylcreem, which made my hair look wet. It felt heavy and overly greasy. It turned out better after I rewashed it and used less. I did some push-ups and sit-ups and shadowboxed in front of the mirror. Then, I flexed my muscles in Bruce's classic pose. My abs didn't look too bad, but my spaghetti arms could, at most, smash a mosquito. I still wasn't sure about my hair. There are times I'd like to have Bruce's hair. And then there are times I'd like the Robert Redford look. Some of the guys at school are doing perms. That would be so cool, but I bet it would turn out looking stupid on me.

Jane banged on the bathroom door to hurry me up. When I came out, she studied me from head to toe.

"Date, huh?"

"Leave me alone." I nudged her aside.

"Do Mama and Baba know you're going out tonight?"

"I'm eighteen. I'm an adult. It's none of your business or theirs." I stepped into my room and was about to close the door when Jane's foot blocked it. She studied the new Bruce poster I'd just put up.

"You know Bruce Lee's a sleazy dirtbag?" She pointed at my posters of him all over my walls.

"What are you talking about?"

"The night he died, he was with a Taiwanese actress. I doubt they were watching reruns of *Get Smart*."

I regretted having a sister and was ready to slam the door on her foot. "You don't know what you're talking about. They were rehearsing."

She giggled. "Sure, they were. Maybe if there was a scene where they get high and shag. I heard he really got around."

"Shag? Where'd you learn that?"

"*Sesame Street*, of course."

"First, watch your mouth. Second, what you said about Bruce is a lie." I had to take a breath and could feel my fists clench. I knew Bruce loved Linda and his family and would never do that.

"If you say so. Hey, can I try some of your Mary Jane?"

"Mary Jane?" I looked around to see if Mama or Baba were around. I guess she knew they weren't.

I grabbed her by the arm, pulled her into my room, and closed the door. "What are you, stupid? Are you trying to get me into trouble? And where did you learn to talk like that? 'Mary Jane,' really?"

She pulled her arm free. "Me, get you into trouble? You don't need help with that. Everyone's using it. Even your hero Bruce Lee did. Just give me some to try, and I'll leave you alone."

I tried to whisper but wound up clenching my teeth. I refused to believe what she was saying about Bruce because it was 100 percent bullshit. "I am not going to give 'Mary Jane' to my little sister. Now buzz off."

"He did more than just smoke weed, I'll bet. Can't you just lose this protective-big-brother routine and be a normal teenage drug dealer?"

I shoved her out of my room and slammed the door. I waited for Bruce to appear with a rebuttal and a put-down of Jane, but he didn't show.

"Friends at school ask if I'm the Egg Roll Sister," she yelled from behind the door. "You might as well let me try some. I can probably help you sell. Nobody would ever suspect me."

For a moment, I wondered if maybe that wasn't such a bad idea. Demand has exceeded delivery capacity. But what have I done? My grade-nine sister and other students her age at Central Commerce High know I'm dealing. That means other nearby schools might know something.

"Dream on, no way." I glanced at the clock and saw that I had to boogie if I didn't want to be late for Angie.

Jane eventually disappeared, but I wasn't sure she'd let it go. Do people at her school really know about me? I'm not sure what makes me madder, her asking for dope or running her mouth about Bruce. I pushed those thoughts away and turned up the music.

Chapter 32

Luke or Han Solo

ANGIE HAD AGREED to meet outside the Uptown Theatre on Yonge and Bloor. Before she showed up, my eye was twitching. It only does that when I'm extremely nervous. I got it under control when she arrived, all made up with dark-cherry lipstick and a foxy outfit with a flowy top, like Stevie Nicks.

I paid for the tickets, two drinks, and a box of popcorn, so we had to share, which (I'm sure she also noticed) made it more like a date.

During the movie, our hands touched when we reached for the popcorn. She shifted her leg a few times so it brushed against mine.

Afterward, she said the whole *Star Wars* experience was visually thrilling. She enjoyed the good-versus-evil story and thought Harrison Ford was a dream. I suggested we go for a slice, but she had to get home to check on her mother. Her face tightened when she talked about her, so I figured she was actually worried and not just blowing me off. She said her mother was sick a lot and had to be watched. I wondered why but didn't want to pry. Angie also shared that she had a part-time job delivering meals at the Wellesley Hospital. She hated it, but they needed the money.

We strolled to the subway so she could have a cigarette. I wished we had time for something to eat, a record-store browse, anything to make the evening go on. Once we entered Bloor-Yonge station, we ran for the southbound train, barely making it, then giggled as we squeezed into our seats.

"Andrew said *Star Wars* will break the box-office record set by *The Sound of Music*," I said.

"Really?" Angie said. "No way, *Star Wars* will never be that popular. But if they make a part two, do you think Princess Leia would get it on with Luke or Han Solo?"

"She goes for Luke, the little guy. They return to Tatooine, turn the moisture farm into a spa, and deliver Chinese food, but no egg rolls."

"And," she wrapped a hand on my arm and squeezed, "Wookiees and all sorts of hairy creatures come from far and wide to eat and relax, leading to interspecies peace and harmony."

Her hand touching my arm excited me. I hoped it didn't show. "Not to mention balance in the universe," I said. "This 'feel the force' thing is kind of weak. But I'd see it."

"Me too," she said.

With me, I hope. I was sad to see my stop come up so fast. She was going all the way to Parkdale. Was I supposed to suggest we do this again or tell her I was ready to go steady? Is this where I should have ignored the crowded subway, kissed her, and maybe slipped in some tongue? I wished a power outage could stop the train and temporarily trap us in the dark tunnel. She'd get spooked and reach for my protection and safety. I'd tell her everything would be okay, that I'd look after her. Maybe then we'd kiss.

"Don't think. Go on, kiss her," Bruce said as he alternated one-armed chin-ups on the overhead grab bar. "Do it."

I took deep breaths and timed my move to get up just before the train stopped. I leaned over her, and just then, another passenger stumbled into us, wrecking my chance. Crap. I got up and made for the door, hiding my disappointment with a big smile.

Bruce jumped off the bars and smacked his forehead.

"That was fun." She nodded.

"Yeah, it was a blast." *Except for the no-kiss part.*

She said she'd see me at school. I already couldn't wait.

I wonder if Angie's thinking about me at the same time. Had I landed the kiss, would she be ready to go steady with me?

I keep thinking about *Star Wars*. It's a lot like Bruce's movies—the same good-versus-evil theme, the underdog taking down the Man. Bruce could've played Obi-Wan Kenobi. He's wise enough. He can stick-fight, so pulling out a lightsaber and showing everyone who's boss, like in that Tatooine bar scene, would've been so him. But I bet they would've cast him as a waiter, meekly bowing to the customers. When I think of it, the only people in *Star*

Wars are white, masked, or androids. I don't think Bruce could have gotten even that crummy part. No wonder he bailed on Hollywood.

When I got home, I peeked into the restaurant and saw it had closed, although a light was still on in the back —probably Baba's. I went upstairs and found Jane dancing to ABBA.

I interrupted her. "Where's Mama?"

"What?" she yelled above the music.

"Mama, where is she?"

"Da maa joek is my guess." Playing mahjong. Jane's song ended. "Kind of a weird evening," she said.

"What do you mean?"

Jane rolled her eyes. "Auntie came in with Leo. I don't know. She was nice and everything. But it was like they were snooping."

"Snooping?"

She shrugged. "Auntie talked to everybody like we were her staff and even walked through the kitchen poking around."

"Mama got pretty uptight, especially when Auntie said she was so happy that the Association made the restaurant possible."

"So?"

She grimaced. "It sounded like a reminder that Mama should never forget her place."

I was impressed that Jane had picked up on that. But then again, she quietly picks up on many things, like my special deliveries. I tried to sound chill about Auntie snooping around. The debt was on its way to being paid off. Why was she scoping us out?

"Auntie said she missed Mama and invited her to come for some games. She laughed and said she'd even let Mama win." Jane paused. "Is Mama in trouble?"

Damn, Jane was too smart for her own good. "No, why would you say that? Mama's fine."

My lie was on its way to being true. I was squaring the debt. "Auntie's just happy that business has picked up for us. She's probably curious."

"Well, Baba was ready to explode. He finally did when Auntie left. He thought Auntie had a lot of nerve to show up like nothing had happened. And he couldn't understand why Mama didn't react."

"What do you mean, *like nothing happened*?"

Jane shrugged. "Parental units—who knows? And the way Barry ran out of here, too."

"What?"

"You know he asked me out?" Jane chuckled.

"He did what?"

"He asked me out. Once I stopped laughing, I told him he was too young for me. Anyway, he went to the washroom, and when he came out, he saw Auntie and Leo and snuck out the back exit. Strange. Do they know each other?"

It was a good question. I shrugged.

Now with Mama going down to the Association again, it'll probably lead to more fighting between her and Baba.

I dialled Barry's place, but there was no answer. His pad was only a short walk over, but I wanted to see how things went with Mama. I tried to stay up but fell asleep waiting. I woke up at four in the morning to Mama's plastic slippers scuffling along our hardwood floors. I jumped out of bed.

"Johnny, did I wake you? Go back to bed."

Her face softened. She must have had a good night at the Association. I hoped Barry was also home and was tempted to call, but I decided to wait. I was pissed at him for ruining the good-vibes buzz I had going after my date.

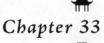

Chapter 33

Mama, Meet Gwai Lo Girl

THE NEXT DAY, Angie and I skipped an afternoon of school. I gave the office a note with Mama's forged signature. *Please excuse Johnny for his absence as his presence is required for family matters which he must attend to. Hence his absence. Yours Truly, Mrs. Wong.*

We jumped on the College streetcar at Bathurst right by my apartment and grabbed two seats in the back. The streetcar lurched forward, then suddenly stopped. I saw Mama running for it. She got on and saw the empty seats in the back right beside us. I froze.

She spied me and Angie together—crap.

"Another PD day, or is it a football game today?" Her broken English was fingernails on a chalkboard to me, and I cringed at Mama's loud, uncoordinated outfit: a red beanie, a fake fur coat, and paisley slacks.

"Gas leak in the main building. They sent us home as a precaution. We're going to Gwartzman's to get Angie some art supplies." I knew Mama wasn't buying any of it, but it was better than saying I was going roller skating with a gwai lo girl.

An awkward silence fell. As Mama was studying me, Angie nudged me, wanting an introduction.

"Mother, this is my *friend*, Angie."

They shook hands.

While I'd stressed that we were friends, part of me hoped Mama didn't believe it, because I wanted more.

I didn't know what I wanted Angie to hear less, Mama speaking in broken English or me in Toisanese. I wasn't ready for Angie to see that side of me. I like being normal and blending in. I just knew Mama was going to blow it for me.

She faced us and asked Angie what her major was.

"Visual arts."

"She's going to college, Mother." I hoped to dull her inevitably judgmental tone.

Mama raised an eyebrow and nodded. She asked me how to say *impressive* in English, which she repeatedly struggled to pronounce, eliciting Angie's smile. Mama apologized for her Chinglish. The two of them together was my worst form of torture. I eyed the emergency-exit window and imagined busting it down, then leaping to freedom with Angie holding on to me. That's how Bruce would do it. Except Bruce never ran from a fight, although Mama might have stared him down.

I know what Mama wanted to ask Angie: Does your mother approve? Does she know you are with someone of another kind? How much money is there in art?

It was like Angie had read Mama's mind. "My mother would rather I take nursing or go to a teachers' college, but she knows none of that matters if I'm unhappy."

"What about your father? What does he think?"

"My parents are separated," Angie said. "I don't really see my dad."

"I see." Mama nodded. She knows a thing or two about separation. "It must be hard. Just by herself, with you. Are there any brothers and sisters?"

"I'm the youngest. My older brother's in the military. My mother's a stay-at-home, but we get by."

"Angie works part-time at Wellesley Hospital, patient services." I wanted Mama to hear the fancy term for delivering meals.

"That hospital is in a rough area. She must worry about you."

"We live in Parkdale. Sirens go by every night. I've seen police kick down doors ... nothing fazes us anymore."

I could see Mama processing this. "Patient services ... sounds like a good job if you do not get into college. It's always good to have a plan B. You never know what could happen. Even the best plan can go awry. You think you have choices, then they go away."

I wondered if she'd ever had a plan B. Were we it?

"Well, I've got the marks, I can apply for financial aid, and I'll keep working. I'll stay on track," Angie said. "An art museum job, my own place, kids and a dog. I've got it all figured out."

Mama nodded, but I didn't know if it was because she was impressed with Angie having her life laid out or if she was just being polite.

"My Johnny can do anything he wants. He will be the best at whatever he does."

Mama is usually pretty stingy with compliments, so I was floored to hear that.

Before getting off the streetcar, I watched a Chinese woman kiss her child and a man. I guessed they were a family. I was glad Mama wouldn't expect anything like that from me before exiting at McCaul. Instead, she just said she'd see me at home. I was in no hurry for that.

Chapter 34

Roller of Dreams

WEEKDAY AFTERNOONS AT the rink are quiet. It's mostly older couples holding hands. We did a few laps before I made a move on Angie. My hand clasped hers—skin on skin, almost like she was waiting for me. Her hand was soft but firm, reminding me of the artist in her. I hope she didn't mind my clammy grip. Is it possible for a single touch to run through your whole body?

I imagined pulling her into me, gently rubbing our noses, sharing a laugh, and kissing. Tongue-on-tongue sounds gross, but I still want to try a French kiss. Our bodies would wrap together before breaking into a perfectly coordinated tango on the rink, like in the Olympics. The Russian and Chinese judges would give us low marks, but the Canadian and American ones would approve.

The older couples who looked so brittle on their skates nodded and smiled at us. I wanted to believe they were cheering us on—today's youth on display, their hope for tomorrow.

We took a break, ordered fries and Cokes, and watched the old-timers.

"Your mother's cute, especially for a Chinawoman," Angie said.

Hearing that should've made me angry and ruined my mood. But I know she didn't mean anything bad. If she did, she wouldn't be out with me. How could she possibly be prejudiced? I said nothing and acted like she'd never said it. Ignore, pretend, deny, dismiss. I stayed on script.

I was glad to see her move the conversation along. "You'd never see my mother on the streetcar or talking to a stranger."

"Really? Why?"

"She's scared of everything outside our door," Angie said. Her mother managed everything within the house: writing cheques, cleaning, and cooking meals. Angie did everything that had to be done outside: shopping, shovelling snow, and work. Even answering the door pushed her mother's capabilities. Angie worried she'd never be able to leave her. I shuddered at the thought of inheriting another messed-up mother if Angie and I married.

"She lived through the war as a kid but never talked about it," Angie said.

Our mothers were of the same generation and grew up in the same war. Mama never shared her experiences, either. But unlike Angie's mother, she could put them behind her and have a different kind of life.

Soon, it was time to work. Before we went our separate ways, I kissed her on her lips, a quick one. Her eyes lit up like she was surprised—but not shocked or offended.

We waved to one another as my streetcar picked up speed. I craned my neck to watch her on the sidewalk. Her smile stayed bright, and she kept waving, which was as good as blown kisses. I can imagine us growing old together like the couples we saw at the rink. She'd become a world-famous artist, and I'd cook for her. She could inspire me to write. There's no room in my fantasy for any mothers.

Chapter 35

What a Girl Wants

TODAY'S CHALKBOARD SAYING was inspired by Angie. I messed around with Tolstoy. I'd love to be able to write like him someday.

> *All through life, we are asleep until we fall*
> *in love—with Chinese food!*

I helped Mama prep for the day and then went to school. When the lunch bell rang, I went to a corner store and got a cute card of Snoopy hugging Woodstock. I wrote *Thinking of you*—thoughtful, but not enough to scare her off. I slipped it into her locker before the afternoon bell.

Tonight, while Mama and I were shutting down the restaurant, she asked how yesterday's shopping went.

I told her we found all our art supplies at Gwartzman's.

She hesitated long enough for me to know I was busted. "Gwartzman's is on Spadina. You got off after."

I was going to feed her some bull but didn't bother.

"She is a nice girl, Johnny."

Whoa, was this my real mother?

She lit a smoke. "She is smart, strong."

"She is. It's hard to find someone like that." I just about jumped into the air.

She took a deep drag and exhaled through her nostrils. "But she is not for you, and you are not for her. You do not know this yet. She will soon—very soon."

And just like that, the air got sucked out of me.

"What do you know? Is it because she's white?" I wanted to say that hadn't stopped her from dating Rollie before Baba returned.

She shook her head. "It is because you are not what she needs, and she is not what you need. She can make choices, Johnny. Do you know how hard it is for a woman to be in that position? I never had that. I still don't. She is already wise enough not to ruin what she has."

That made me furious. What did she know about anything? "How do you know what she needs? You just met her."

"I am your mama, and I know what you have to give up to have a future, and even then, nothing is certain."

"What future? You mean delivering combos for the rest of my life?"

"I never said that. I want you to finish school. Whatever you want after that is up to you. We can look after the restaurant and ourselves. We don't need you to do that."

Oh yes, you do. "Seriously, what would you do without me?"

"I am your mother, and you are not hearing me. I never said to work in the restaurant. That is your baba's dream for you."

I hate it when she reminds me that she's my mother, as if she'd ever let me forget. Why doesn't she tell me *what she wants*? I wasn't going to stand there and find out. I stormed upstairs, leaving her to finish closing.

Chapter 36

The Model Sister

AFTER SCHOOL, I was chilling out in my room before what I knew would be a busy Halloween night. I really wanted to see Angie at Carlos's bash. She no longer felt like a long shot for me.

Baba stormed in. "It's Jane, your sister ..."

As if I didn't know who she was.

His tight fists dug into his hips. "Her school called. She was caught with drugs. Can you believe this?"

My stomach knotted, and there was no hiding my confusion and concern. I half expected the police to come charging in with guns drawn, looking for me.

What a stupid little shit, that Jane. What was she doing? Had she gotten into my stash? She knew a lot, maybe everything. Her interest in scoring a sample from me should have alerted me that she was up to something. I had an urge to count my stash. The car stayed in the locked garage behind the restaurant all day. It wasn't used for anything except deliveries. I emptied it every night and hid the drugs in the rafter behind a board until the next evening. She could have gotten the other keys from Baba, but she'd have to have been sneaky about it. Easy peasy for her.

"The police arrested her." He smacked my nightstand with his fist. "I have to go to the police station. I hope no one we know sees us. I cannot believe this. There was another girl, a bad influence. It must be the other girl's drugs. Our Jane was framed. I'm going now. Go help your mama downstairs."

As soon as he left, I made for the garage. I looked around before I unlocked the door and entered. I pulled the stash down from the rafter and counted the bags. It was short five dimes. Either Barry or I had miscounted, or Jane had gotten into it. Or Barry had given it to her. If the stupid shit had, I was done with him. I would kick his ass or at least die trying.

I had no idea how to get her and me out of this. Meanwhile, Barry had taken off somewhere, which made me fume. With the police now involved, we had to stop the deliveries and get the weed off our property. Until then, I searched for a different hiding spot, wishing I had something more than a garage to choose from. I found a shovel, dug a small hole in the dirt floor, and covered the bags with dirt and a spare tire.

Baba brought Jane back from the precinct to the restaurant later in the evening. He shuffled in with his shoulders hunched and sat on a stool. I served coffee to some customers and noticed more wrinkles and bags under his eyes. He threw his keys down and raised his voice at me. "This is your fault."

Oh shit, Jane talked. I lost my breath and could feel my heart beating. Several customers looked up from their meals at me. I eyed the door, expecting the police to charge in. Jane kept her head down.

"You are the eldest. It's your job to watch her, to keep her out of trouble."

I lowered my head as if I were still a little boy, ready to be whacked. "Yes, Baba."

"You should watch her friends, too, to weed out the bad seeds and rotten influences. Your sister is young and impressionable and she is easily taken advantage of. You have to do better."

Huh? Her friends? Baba wasn't blaming me for anything other than not screening out Jane's friends. That meant Jane hadn't said anything about me.

He said Jane was charged with possessing drugs.

"I didn't know anything about the drugs," she pleaded, fighting back crocodile tears. "My friend bought it from some Central Tech students. She panicked when she saw the vice principal coming and stuffed it in my bag. I didn't know what was going on."

"Is this true, Johnny? Do boys from your school deal drugs there?"

I glared at Jane from the corner of my eye. "I've never heard of anyone dealing there." It was no secret that CTS students cruised nearby schools, but I wasn't about to tell him.

Mama came in from the kitchen but said nothing while Baba ranted about Jane having to find better friends and maybe changing schools next semester. Even with Jane screwing up, Baba made it seem like it was on me. My failure was a bad reflection on all of us. I apologized and said I'd watch her more carefully.

"I could transfer far away from CTS," Jane said. "There must be schools without drug problems, right, dai goh?" She faked a hopeful look at me.

I should have been madder that she was trying to psych me out, but I was too relieved that she was such a good con and keeping me and the restaurant safe for now.

"CTS is a good school," I said. "It's more than just those creeps."

Baba nodded. "That other student is a bad seed. You must stay away from her."

"Did anyone see you with the police?" Mama asked with arms crossed.

"Probably," Jane replied. "There were other students around. And teachers."

"Then you have embarrassed us again. If people talk and business goes down, it is because of you." Mama pointed at Jane, who predictably started to cry.

It was a bit harsh and dramatic, but that's Chinese parenting, especially once shame has entered the building.

By "again," I assume Mama meant when Jane started that fire.

"See what you have done?" Baba, having fallen for Jane's ploy, shot Mama a look of disgust. Then he lost it, jabbing his finger at Mama as he raised his voice in Toisanese. "She has done nothing wrong. Why are you always so hard on her? You blame her for everything and over nothing."

Mama jabbed right back and yelled even louder. "Why? Why are you so stupid? You think she is an angel who can do no wrong. You are blind. She has a drug charge now. That is not nothing. She could go to jail."

"You are overreacting," Baba said. "She explained everything to the police."

"Am I overreacting? At least I am not blind. She was raised without a mama. She knows nothing and is useless. She brings drugs and the police into our lives. She disgraces us, and it's not her fault? Then whose?"

"Like you are an angel who has done no wrong." Baba said that slowly as if to add emphasis. "Like you have no secrets. Have you brought no indignity onto your family?"

Now, everyone in the restaurant stopped to watch the fight. They didn't need a translator to know this was not about food. I pushed my parents and Jane into the kitchen, startling our part-time dishwasher.

But a setting change didn't slow them down, and Baba continued to fire back. "Why don't you be a real mama for a change? She is Johnny's sister."

"Who are you to lecture me about parenting? The man disappears on his son and suddenly returns with a burden I am supposed to care for. Funny, you are a funny guy. A lousy businessman, a horrible husband, and an absent baba, but a funny guy. Hahahahaha. Tell me when to stop laughing, funny man."

"I came back to try again. Johnny needed a man in his life. I am here to stay. Can you say the same? Your mind is always elsewhere. Do you want to be here with your family or not?"

I stared at Mama, waiting for her reply. She hesitated just long enough to look guilty. "I never said I was going away. You are putting words in everybody's ears."

Baba grabbed Mama's arm. His voice softened. "Let him go. The past is the past. Why torture yourself again and again?"

Who the hell is *him*?

Jane turned around and walked to the back exit. I followed, leaving our parents to duke it out. I yanked her arm before she could make it onto the back stairs up to our rooms. "Did Barry give you the drugs?"

"Ewww. I don't need Barry to score drugs."

"Then why the hell were you stealing from me? What are you, stupid?"

She jerked her arm free and shot me an icy stare. "I just walked away from one argument and will do it again. You can watch if you want." She climbed the stairs. I leaped up behind her.

"That's such a Baba move. Stir up the pot, then run away and leave other people stuck with your crap." *Like dumping a half sister on me*, I almost said. "And why did you have to say they were CTS boys? Now the police will be searching my school."

"Because creepy CTS boys are always cruising our halls and streets, hunting for girls, proudly pointing to their stupid Adidas shirts and saying 'All Day I Dream About Sex.' Maybe now someone will make them stop. Besides, if you're not bringing weed to school, you have nothing to worry about. Are you?"

"Of course not. I'm not an idiot."

"You are," she said. "I never asked you to bring drugs into this stupid family. By the way, you're welcome for me not ratting you out."

She stopped me with that. She had protected me and our family. I have to give her that. She climbed the stairs and then slammed her door. It didn't take long for her to crank up her music to full volume. From below, the muffled yells of my parents drifted up. I sank onto a step and collapsed.

How could I ever have thought I could hold my family together?

Chapter 37

The Chinese Casanova

EVEN WITHOUT JANE'S drama, Halloween night was going to be crazy. Food and weed orders came in fast over the phone, which wouldn't stop ringing, and every seat in the restaurant was taken. A couple of trick-or-treaters came in wearing Wookiee masks. Baba begrudgingly gave them fortune cookies.

I had real reservations about continuing with the deliveries. First, I needed to talk to Barry, wherever he was. I figured he was partying at Ayeisha's. I tried to slow down the weed orders and only took small ones, telling everyone else we were out. Meanwhile, Mama and Baba silently worked around each other while Jane remained in her room.

Mama told me that Andrew had called and that he'd sounded upset. I'm sure he was being a drama queen again, so I ignored him. Instead, I found Angie's mother's phone number in the white pages. No one answered at first. I tried again, and someone picked up, probably her mother. "Hello?" She sounded unfriendly, so I hung up. After a quick delivery, I phoned again. This time, Angie picked up. She asked how I got her number and why I was calling. After I told her I needed to talk about Jane, she listened.

She suggested I give Jane space, lay off the "big brother knows best" lecture, and let her work it out.

I wasn't sure I could do that. I tried to explain that there was more at stake than a possession charge. Jane had made our family look like lowlifes. On top of that, she'd highlighted my failure as the eldest.

The shame angle is an invisible anvil that Mama keeps ready to drop on us anytime. Occasionally, I'll get a "Don't be stupid" or "I disown you." Jane gets slightly different twists from her: "... because you had no mama to teach you, that's why you're so fat" or "you have no manners, no culture ... you're acting like a homeless person." She calls us both useless. Sometimes, she'll double up on her combo of put-downs, like she's trying to get good value from her insults. Like, "You're fat and useless," which is more often for Jane, who's never been fat. Things used to be worse long ago when Mama was drinking more.

"That's interesting," Angie said. "In a way, it's like me. With my mom needing all this help, I wonder if I'll ever get to live my life."

"That's exactly it. I live for the family, to keep face, and my job is to protect them."

"From who?"

"Themselves, really. They're screw-ups. Without me, they'd be a disaster."

"There's lots I don't get," Angie said. "Like, why is Jane's mess also yours?"

It was too complicated to explain. But it was great just talking with her like she was mine.

I had a quick delivery to a new weed customer on Albany Avenue, south of Dupont. They also wanted two combos with extra rice and a special order of beef with bitter melon. Albany's less rich-looking than Palmerston but has a similar column of old trees. The last of their red, yellow, and orange autumn leaves were hanging on in the late afternoon sun. In the small lawn for 241 Albany, a girl's bicycle lay on its side. It had a torn banana seat and high-rise handlebars with streamers.

I rang the doorbell. A girl a little younger than Jane, dressed in a Princess Leia costume, opened the door.

There was no way I would hand over three dimes to her. I looked around for an adult. Much to my relief, I heard a woman asking who it was.

"The Chinese food man," the little girl yelled back.

A girl around my age came out in a Farrah Fawcett wig that didn't make her look anything like Farrah Fawcett. "Smells great. How much?"

"Uhmm, I just want to make sure this is the right order." I recited the order, leaving out the egg rolls.

"We also ordered three egg rolls with mustard. Her dad loves his mustard." She smiled and shrugged her shoulders.

"You sure?" I double-checked.

She nodded.

"Okay, $37.60."

She pulled out two twenties, thanked me, and closed the door. That was a nice tip. I remember those.

By cutting back on deliveries, I was probably disappointing lots of Halloween parties. But I did make a very special delivery to Angie's place. Her street in Parkdale was crawling with puny Darth Vaders and Princess Leias.

I banged on her door again and again. Someone inside told me to go away. It must have been Angie's mother. I said I was a friend dropping off something for Angie. It was a rose, dumplings, and noodles. I felt like a Chinese Casanova. I left them by the door.

Chapter 38

Guilty

GETTING READY FOR school, I didn't have to fight Jane for the bathroom. Her door remained closed all morning, which was fine because I mostly didn't want to deal with her. Part of me wanted to thank her for not ratting me out, but another part wanted to yell at her for not minding her own business. With the cops involved yesterday and visions of getting busted dancing in my head last night, I'd had trouble sleeping.

I'd dreamed Gregory Peck as Atticus Finch defended me in court. He held a news conference surrounded by reporters from the *Chinese Times*, *Sing Tao Daily*, and my father's favourite, *Ming Pao*. Peck's tall frame completely obscured me from the reporters. He said nothing about me or my family. Instead, he spewed menu items in Chinglish. No one seemed to mind. The reporters put their cameras and notepads away and basked in his presence.

I woke up knowing I had to stop the weed deliveries immediately. I was ready to make that call without Barry. He'd be pissed as all hell.

Baba needed help with the breakfast shift, so I almost missed running into Angie on her way to her morning art class. She was walking from the streetcar stop at Bathurst and Harbord like she was on a mission. I called out to her as she stepped on the school grounds.

Her ocean-blue eyes shot flames at me. "Was that you who came by my house last night?"

I lowered my head, held my breath, and nodded as my stomach sank with dread.

"Not cool. And was it you who was phoning and hanging up?"

I nodded again.

"You scared the crap out of my mother. She was up all night, and me with her."

I couldn't say sorry, not because I wasn't, but because it would be like explaining how you peed yourself. Nothing was going to cut it.

We saw Carlos cross the street from Nick's. She ran to him, leaving me naked with embarrassment.

I had a rotten day at school. I kept thinking of Angie and wondering if the cops were going to sweep through with police dogs who'd sniff weed residue all over me.

By three-thirty p.m., the low dark clouds already made it look like evening. Dead leaves clung to skeletal trees, waiting for their inevitable downward flight. I hung outside the art building to see if Angie would come out, wanting a chance to explain. Instead, Carlos, in his unbuttoned CTS varsity jacket, made a straight line for me, his fists clenched at his side.

I tried to play it cool and look cocky, like Bruce.

"Stay away from Angie, you hear me?" He was in big-brother mode.

I put my hands on my hips. "Why? Is there a problem?"

He didn't bother to answer. His right hook to my stomach knocked my wind out and left me on my side, arms wrapped around my stomach, gasping for air. It stunned me the way falling off the monkey bars used to as a kid. You think you're going to die and that you've sucked your last breath. It's the longest twenty or thirty seconds of your life. But then the air returns in short, tiny breaths.

Through closed eyes, fighting back tears, I heard him walk away.

I thought of Andrew. He might not know an allegory from a metaphor, but he'd have taken the hit for me. Yet I couldn't even return his calls.

I wished I had Bruce's abs of rippling steel.

"They're remarkable, aren't they?" Bruce held a *V* ab pose while quietly reading a copy of *Tao Te Ching*, shirtless, his abs glistening. He could've taken a dropkick to the gut and not bat an eye. But I'm not him, and I'd gotten whipped like he'd never been.

"Piss off, Bruce, just piss off."

I remained on my side for several minutes, feeling sorry for myself. I remember Bruce saying it's not wrong to be knocked down but that it's important to ask why. Reflection shows hope. Well, I'd gotten my ass kicked because Carlos is way bigger, and I'd strayed into forbidden territory—dreaming big. Is that reflection enough? Because I don't see any hope.

I crept home like an old man. When I got there, Mama said Angie had just come by. That straightened me up.

"She waited for you. Then she left a note."

I wasn't sure if Mama was about to lecture me on the dangers of white women or if she was just curious. She had that "I told you so" look, but then her face slackened, and I sensed something maternal, almost like she wanted to shield me. As if. I silently waited for her to buzz off until she got the hint and went to serve a customer.

Sitting at the counter, I tore open the envelope. Maybe Angie wanted to straighten things out. Maybe she'd heard about Carlos jumping me, felt bad, and was ready for us to officially go out.

I unfolded her letter.

Johnny,

I'm sorry I was so mean this morning. I hadn't slept and was mad at you and myself. I should have started by thanking you for the food, the rose, and all the notes you stuffed in my locker. I wish going to school and just life wasn't so complicated. I have too much other shit going on, like looking after my mother and just getting out of school in one piece. I don't have time or energy for more. I'm sorry we can't be friends or anything else. You're a nice guy, really you are. Maybe it'll be different when the Luke and Leia Reunited *movie comes out. Perhaps we'll both be in different spaces but on the same planet.*

Daughter of de Lempicka

I reread the letter, then crumpled it. She's so stupid. They'll never make another *Star Wars* movie.

We can't be friends or anything else. You're a nice guy, really you are ... but you're Oriental, a 130-pound weakling, you deliver Chinese food, and your mama speaks like she just got off the boat.

Everything else going on around me blurred. I screamed in my head—*What a lowlife, scheming scumsucker!* I cradled my head in the crook of my arm, resting it on the counter. For how long, I don't know. I replayed our dates, the things I'd said, ruminating over what I could have done differently. I imagined taking Leo's rusty steel pipe to Carlos's kneecap. Angie had said I was different, and she liked that. Too different? Had the smell of our food gotten to her? Had she imagined having to put up with Mama?

Dishes clanked in the kitchen. Mama was thanking one of the regulars for coming in.

I took a deep breath. I was mad at myself for ever thinking I had a shot at her. Then, I got pissed again at her. It was her loss. Her stupid art and white-picket-fence dreams were just ridiculous. It was lucky I hadn't gotten caught up in her fairyland. I didn't need her or any of that fantasy. If she hadn't done this, I would've gotten smart and dumped her anyway. Maybe Barry and my parents were right. I should date my kind, and when Barry finally turns up, I'm going to ask for Sheila's or Sherry's—whatever her name's—phone number.

I wanted to slam the counter and scream. Instead, I told Mama I wasn't feeling good and had to sleep.

Bruce says defeat is not defeat unless accepted as a reality in your mind. That's a pretty idiotic thing to say, because the reality is I got my ass kicked and my heart dumped, and no fortune cookie saying is going to change that.

Chapter 39

Forgetting My Place

I STRUGGLED TO get out of bed the next morning.

"Bruce, you never got your ass kicked, so humiliation would be a new thing for you. Well, I'm here to teach *you* something for a change. Humiliation is wanting to crawl into crevices where cockroaches live and die because that's where you belong. If not that, disappear, be invisible, start all over. It's like someone's hollowed out your insides and left them on the sidewalk where anybody can stomp their dog poop-crusted Kodiaks on them. And then, you still have to go to school before working at a Chinese restaurant.

"Not true, my friend. I know what humiliation is," Bruce said as he unleashed several spinning heel kicks. "When I pitched my Warrior series to Warner Bros., they rejected it. Then they turned around and made my Warrior series but renamed it *Kung Fu*—casting David Carradine, a white actor, in a Chinese role. Assholes."

"That sucked, but I loved that show," I said.

"Glad you think so. It was humiliating, like every time I was offered roles as a humble, kowtowing servant.

So, I know what you are talking about, my friend. But I also know how to use it." He tapped his head.

I dragged myself to school, hoping to run into Andrew and that he'd talk to me again. More than anything else, I needed to just hang with him. I hadn't told him about Angie, Barry, weed, anything. I'm good at talking about school, the Leafs, and the rigged pinball machines, but we never dive deeper. It's like we've had a silent agreement to keep things light. And that was okay. Except now, maybe I needed to break that agreement.

Only losers get dumped by mail, which is what Angie did to me, even if her letter was hand-delivered. I was so close. I could tell she was into me. Then, *bam*, I was out, just like in wrestling when they do a Greco-Roman flip. To add to my headache, Barry's AWOL. Plus, my parents have taken their fights to a whole new level, and my sister might be charged for possession, thanks to me. At least it's not a trafficking charge.

A few students gave me a nod, but most ignored me, like before I started moving weed. I figured Carlos was spreading the word that I was a nimrod.

I was glad to see Andrew down the crowded hallway. I hadn't called him back, but figured we could just talk in person. As the herd of students scattered to homeroom, he turned, revealing a bruised face and split lip.

"Andrew, what the hell—?"

Baahir stepped out from behind Andrew. He was also bruised, even worse. They walked away from me toward class.

"Hey, what happened? What's going on?" I scurried beside them.

"Well, look at what the cat just dragged in." There was no hiding Andrew's tone.

"What's with the attitude, man? I only asked what happened."

"Like you care," he said without looking at me.

"Of course I do. What happened?"

"We got jumped."

"What ... by who?"

He stopped. "Last night, I was supposed to pick you up to stake out the studio and wait for Rush. But my car broke down on the way to your place. I called and called, thinking you could pick us up. I left messages. Your old lady said you were out. I guess you weren't home waiting for us like you said you would be."

Of course, the Halloween Rush.

"You forgot, didn't you?"

My silence said it all.

"We were stuck on Bathurst when Domenic and his goons, stoned out of their minds, went on a Paki-bashing and cornered us. There were too many of those assholes. As you can see, we're not so pretty anymore."

I didn't know what to say. What could I say? I had messed up. I felt like I'd just got my gut kicked in again, but this time, I deserved it. "Did you get a couple shots in, at least?"

"Baahir fought like a beast and put one of those goons down."

Baahir and Andrew traded some skin.

"What does it matter now?" Baahir said. "We are not your concern anymore, Johnny." That was the first time Baahir had ever held my gaze. His big dark eyes filled with disappointment.

"Yeah, you've got the goon squad now, and you're dealing dope." The disgust on Andrew's face was obvious. "You don't need us."

Damn, he knew. I wanted to disappear into a hole. What a loser friend I was.

"You think I don't know anything?" He looked down on me.

I shook my head. "Look, I messed up. I'm sorry, okay? Things are really bad right now. Can we just be good again?"

I could tell he thought about it. He was usually so laid-back. For sure, he was going to let it go. I just knew it. But he and Baahir just shook their heads and walked off like I was dead to them. I deserved that.

I shared two classes with them, but they ignored me. Then I got mad and thought what assholes. Screw them, I don't need them. I don't need Angie or anyone. I don't care. Who wants to hang with people going nowhere? They were bringing me down anyway. The whole day was a bummer. I was cranky, the teachers were cranky, the students were cranky, thanks to the latest Leafs game.

I endured a long lecture on chemical systems and equilibrium during the last period. I stayed awake, imagining myself whipping together an acid bomb and lighting up Carlos's Monte Carlo. I'd get busted, and there'd be a trial.

Darth Vader would be the prosecuting attorney. I wouldn't be allowed to speak in my defence, but Gregory Peck, as Atticus Finch, would be my attorney.

"Your Honour," Atticus leaps out of his chair, pauses and takes out his handkerchief, then removes his glasses, which he wipes, "it was only a simple lips-to-lips kiss, lasting microseconds. My unscrupulous but humble client did no more than any other teenager, even an Oriental, would do, given the temptation. My client merely broke a rigid and time-honoured code of our society, a code so severe that whoever breaks it is hounded. The code of coveting something you cannot have."

When Carlos gets on the stand, I call him a meathead who can't spell his name without cheating. The courtroom gasps as Carlos stands and calls me a liar, then spells out his name to cheers from the gallery. The judge bangs the gavel to silence everyone before holding me in contempt for slander and for forgetting that Carlos quarterbacked the senior football team. The jurors shake their heads at me in disapproval. I lean into Atticus and say I'm ready to do the time. That I deserve it. Atticus hushes me. He's been rehearsing for his moment and doesn't want to mess it up.

In his closing summation, he squints at each of the jurors. "I am confident that you gentlemen will review, without prejudice, the evidence you have heard, come to a decision, and restore this ... this," he wipes his glasses again before looking at me, "this Oriental to his family. In the name of God, do your duty."

The jury of all white men don't need to go off and deliberate. They find me guilty of forgetting my place and then they squabble about where to order Chinese food. The judge says justice will be served: I'll deliver food forever, keeping quiet except to thank customers for ordering from the Red Pagoda.

The dismissal bell went off, and the students tore out of class. I didn't want to talk to anybody, so I made for the door.

But Mr. Miller found me. I figured he was going to ride me about that college application again. He led me to his office. "Johnny, you know I believe in you."

I expected another "you can go to college" speech. Instead, he looked pissed as he reached into his desk and pulled out a baggie with three dime bags inside. "This was in our food order, which you delivered to our house—241 Albany."

My heart plummeted: two combos with extra rice and beef with bitter melon and three egg rolls … with mustard. A $2.40 tip.

"Our babysitter is a dimwit. She thought nothing of giving you forty dollars for my eight-dollar order of food, and it turns out, three bags of marijuana."

I blinked and held my breath.

"Suppose my daughter had opened it up?"

"I just delivered, sir. I don't know anything about this."

"You took the money. You knew exactly what you were doing."

"We have some new staff. Maybe they messed up?"

"Johnny, don't play me. Lots of kids are dealing drugs these days. I have to frisk you. We'll either call the police or speak to your parents, probably both. I haven't decided which yet." He shook his head and got up. "By the way, you're blowing this. I had a partial scholarship in the works for you."

He didn't have to call me a loser. I could do that for him.

"I don't know what you were thinking or if your parents are involved. But you could all go to jail, your restaurant could close, you—"

"No, they have nothing to do with this." That was the truth. I had to protect them.

He made me empty my pockets, roll down my socks, and take off my shoes and show him the insides. I had nothing on me, but he marched me to my locker and made me open it. Several students watched from a distance, gaping the way people do at a car accident.

A bunch of overdue novels burst out from my locker onto our feet.

He picked up Bruce's *Tao of Jeet Kune Do*. "Now there's a tragic character. Do you ever imagine what Lee could have been like if he wasn't a drug addict? Maybe he'd be alive today."

He may as well have cursed my mother. "Sir, how can you say that?"

"Come on, Johnny—wine, women, and hash brownies, which were his favourite, if rumours are true. None of them are saints. Writing this"—Mr. Miller held up Bruce's book—"doesn't mean he was any different. For all anyone knows, he was high the whole time he wrote it."

Bruce did a spinning kick within an inch of Mr. Miller's face. "What a jerk. He obviously doesn't understand the artistic process. Plus, I didn't drink."

"Exactly," I replied to Bruce.

"I'm glad you see it that way," Mr. Miller said. "Sometimes it's not so much that our legends deceive us—it's how we deceive ourselves."

"What a pretentious jerk," Bruce said.

I couldn't spit out what I wanted to say. I wanted Mr. Miller to go away and leave me alone, but it wasn't going to be that easy. "I owe money to some people."

He looked skeptical. "To whom?"

I bit the inside of my cheek. My intuition was telling me that someone was making a run for our restaurant.

"Some people, that's all I can say. I'm trying to get out of trouble. It's not what you think, sir."

"That's pretty vague, Johnny." He wasn't buying any of it. I don't blame him. He placed his hands on his hips. "This stops now."

"It will, sir. I have to ... those people will come after our restaurant. It's our livelihood. It's everything to my parents."

"Are you saying your family's in danger?"

I saw a chance to slow him down. "Only if I don't pay these people off. And if they find out I said something to an outsider, there will be even more trouble."

"I can be trusted, Johnny, believe me."

"I do, sir. But I couldn't tell you about this because I wasn't sure you would understand."

I could see him thinking.

"It's board policy for me to contact the police and the principal," he said.

"But I didn't do anything on school property. I would never. I never brought anything to school." That was true, at least. "Besides, once the police get involved, we're finished."

"Are you saying you're in danger?"

Of losing the restaurant, for sure. Of getting blown up like that place on Elizabeth Street, where people had been injured and killed? That depended on the triad. Who knew if they wanted to make another statement to the community? My parents could be next. What if they turned on the stove one morning, and the whole building went up in flames?

"I hope there's no danger, sir. But I really don't know."

He studied me like he was probing for the lie. Then his gaze hovered around the hallway, landing momentarily on a few guys cursing. They stopped once they saw Mr. Miller staring them down. His attention returned to me.

"Alright, but I will speak with your parents. I need to know this is going to stop."

"Wait. Give me a couple of days before you call them. Please, Mr. Miller."

He shook his head. "No can do."

Taking a page from Jane's playbook, I choked up. The tears came easily. I just had to think of us being arrested, losing the restaurant, disappointing my parents. All of us winding up in jail. My chest heaved. I wanted to disappear. "Please, sir."

My begging had softened him. "Alright, Johnny. You have two days. But I want you to check in with me tomorrow. Then I'm calling. I'm disappointed in you. This is not who you are. I still think you have a future."

I don't know why his disappointment in me felt like a roundhouse kick to my chest. Maybe because he actually believed I could get that scholarship and go to college.

When I returned to the restaurant, Mama and Baba were looking at new menu designs. I was glad they were talking again, amicably. They asked for my opinion.

"Can we afford this?" I said. "What's wrong with what we have? Maybe we shouldn't be looking at making any changes." I almost said that we should just sell everything and get out.

Mama put the designs down and glared at me.

"For months, you say we should update our menu and replace items that are not selling, that we are wasting stock that is not moving. Now you say what is wrong with the old menu?"

I shrugged. "Sales are up. Maybe it's not a good time to try something different."

"First, *you* said try something different," Baba said. "That is what I am doing. Besides, sales are up because of specific items. You deliver all the time. You know this."

They turned back to the designs.

"My vice principal might call soon," I blurted out.

They exchanged stressed looks. A school calling is only a little less scary for them than the police coming by, especially after Jane just got busted at school.

"Why? What have you done?"

I didn't know what to say at first. "Mr. Miller placed an order last night ..."

"Yes?"

"Two combos, beef with—"

"What is it, Johnny?"

"He ... also had egg rolls ... the bitter melon."

Baba stared right into me. "Yes, beef with bitter melon—special order. What's wrong? Did he get sick?"

"No, no. He loved it. He thought it was amazing. He might call."

"For another order?" Baba asked.

"No ... he found out we were the owners. He wants to ask if we'll donate food for the year-end senior football team dinner."

"A donation? That means our expense. How many people?"

"Yes, for free. There are about thirty. They're nice guys, really. Oh, plus the coaches, trainers, mascots, cheerleaders."

"Does he think we're Lichee Garden? We're not rich. No."

"You sure, Baba?"

"Of course. How can we say no without offending him?"

"Just don't take his call. If he comes by, keep yourself busy. He needs to connect with you soon, within a week. If he doesn't, he'll find somebody else. We can apologize, send him a complimentary combo."

Baba liked that idea. I'd bought myself a few more days to devise another plan.

"What happened to Barry?" Mama asked.

No one had seen him since last week, but Barry taking off for a couple of days to party it up at Ayeisha's wasn't unusual.

I said I'd heard he wasn't feeling well and would check on him. I tried phoning him and again got no answer. And the weed orders kept coming in. I told them we were out of mustard. I decided without Barry to suspend sales. Things were getting out of control. The last thing I needed was for Mr. Miller to test me out to try to catch me still dealing.

I pounded on Barry's door between takeout deliveries, but no one answered. Maybe he was stoned somewhere or at his girlfriend's. I left a note in capital letters, saying he needed to call.

Chapter 40

The Big Order

MAMA TOOK THE afternoon off work, so I did the same from school. She said nothing about that.

We must have received twenty delivery orders in the first two hours, almost all for dinners and egg rolls with mustard, and nearly all were repeat customers. Again, I said we were sold out of mustard. They got the hint but asked when we'd have more. I thought of the remaining stash, most of which was covered in dirt beneath the garage floor. There was still a lot to push, but it was already decided—I was out.

Then I got an order for fifty-six egg rolls with mustard and nothing else from an apartment on Stephanie Street. That was two ounces, quite a party. It would make an unreal final order before walking away for good.

This big order got Mama's attention after our egg roll orders had cratered the last two days.

She double-checked the unfamiliar address. "What's going on, Johnny?"

I shrugged. "We have two hundred egg rolls in the freezer. We need to move them."

"They will keep, and we will use them. But don't take this order," she said with a wary look. "I don't have a good feeling about it."

A good feeling? Mama never talked like that.

"We don't need this," she said. "Tell them we are sold out."

I was still annoyed with her for what she'd said about Angie not needing me. So, just to piss her off, I took the order and walked away before she could get a word in.

I hurried to Barry's, looked around for cops first, then knocked repeatedly. A light was on inside. I turned the doorknob and pushed the door open. In the kitchen, his weight scale and boxes of baggies lay on the counter.

I called out, but there was no reply. His furniture was turned over. Bottles and dishes lay smashed and scattered over the floor. I tensed up, thinking he'd been beaten up, half expecting to find him lying in a pool of blood. I hoped he'd only been B&E'd. I hoped whoever had done it was gone. But his stereo was still there, as was the TV, but it, too, was smashed. I picked up an empty bottle and held it by the neck like a hammer before entering the bedroom. I hoped he was blacked out drunk and passed out on his bed.

The bed was empty. A ceiling tile had been ripped down. I climbed on the bed and peered into the dark opening, guessing Barry had hidden his stash there. He probably still had his three pounds, as long as he hadn't smoked it all. But Barry wasn't around and I couldn't figure out if he'd made a quick escape or what.

I locked up behind me. I didn't know what else to do, so I made out for the Stephanie Street delivery. It had started to rain. The slick roads made my worn tires hydroplane. I parked in the visitors' and looked up at the concrete high-rise, a brooding twenty-five-storey behemoth overlooking Grange Park. I wished I hadn't accepted the order. It meant leaving the car for a long time while I went to the twenty-first floor. Plus, there was no quick, easy escape. I told myself I was feeling paranoid for no reason.

I rang the intercom and was immediately buzzed in. The cold, empty lobby smelled of rich curry, fried onions, and soggy socks. A child was crying, and muffled sounds in different languages came from all directions.

The elevator was plastered with ads for dry cleaning, pizza joints, and hair salons. I made a mental note to advertise the Red Pagoda here, then realized if I were to do that, I'd have to return. I exited on the twenty-first floor and found the apartment. Maybe I was stressed out for nothing and just needed to chill.

The door opened before I even knocked.

"Red Pagoda delivery."

A big guy with a bad perm and acne asked me to come in.

I hesitated and wondered where I'd seen him before. "That won't be necessary. It'll be $480, please." I raised the big brown paper bag.

Then, I remembered. He was the triad soldier at our restaurant who'd talked to Leo. I backed away with the bag in my hand, but he grabbed me by the collar and pulled me inside. I stumbled on a thin carpet, almost falling, and he slammed the door.

"Nay ho, Johnny," Auntie said from a recliner by the window.

Despite the situation, the familiarity of her voice was calming. Out of habit, I half bowed and replied, "Ah yi," and asked what she was doing there.

Someone came up behind me, grabbed the bag, and smacked the back of my head. Luckily for me, there wasn't much force behind it. "Stupid," Leo said.

The Buddha Boy soldier grabbed the bag of egg rolls. He emptied its contents onto a coffee table. Egg rolls spilled out, as did a mound of little baggies of weed. He opened one of them and sniffed, then nodded to Auntie.

"Everyone says my product is exceptional," she said in English before taking a heavy drag of her cigarette.

"Your product?" I shook my head and quickly thought things through. I knew she ran the games at the Association and made sure debts were paid. But dealing drugs? Since when?

"Hai lo ... of course. It belongs to me. And I want it back now."

"No, it's ours. I have contacts." I heard a moan from another room. "What's that?" I said in Toisanese.

"A contact?" She said, chuckling. "A thieving cockroach, you mean? We've been thinking of branching out and feeling our way around. You've created an interesting business model. You've proved that money can be made. But first, cockroaches must be crushed, both the two- and six-legged kinds. And once I do that, I can see having many more depots like your shithole of a restaurant." She flattened her cigarette into an overflowing plate of butts.

I switched to English. "Excuse me, ah yi, but I don't understand how my business concerns you. I am a simple small operator."

She chuckled. "You're right. This is business, and you are in way over your head. You are operating with stolen goods, my goods, boldly and stupidly taken from our Association basement. Do you know that your partner is a thief?"

I blinked with surprise. I knew none of that.

"A neighbour saw a boy with golden hair sneaking out of our basement window. He made off with our property. It wasn't until the fool started handing samples out like Halloween candy that we traced it to the Pagoda. We have been watching you. Once we saw him slipping out the back door of the Pagoda, we knew we had our man. I had to see how much you knew and how you were running things. Impressive."

My fingers balled into a fist.

"Nevertheless, you are here, and all but one question remains."

"I didn't steal from you."

"I believe you. Trust me, Johnny, you don't want to steal from us. You still have your fingers because you are family. You know your place. You are bright and capable, not foolhardy and reckless like this gwai lo. Of the five pounds that were stolen, we recovered just under three pounds from the Golden Boy's apartment. You and he will now reimburse me."

So, Auntie and her boys were the ones who'd broken into Barry's apartment. My shoulders slumped. "But I've already given you over two grand."

"That was for your mama's debt. Which you shrewdly convinced me to defer. I am soft for you because you are so smart. But you will return the rest of my property. With these two ounces, you still have yaat bong." She raised a finger for *one pound*. "The Golden Boy told us you sold a pound. You did well. I'm impressed. I want all the money from what you sold, plus interest."

"You wanted to help. You said you were worried about Mama."

"I do want to help. But it's you I worry about. Your mother stopped being sensible long ago. I have shed many tears over her. You have no idea." I caught her glance at Leo. "But once you leave that mess, I still have much hope for you."

I shook my head.

"This is business, and I have been very patient with your mother."

If she was going after our restaurant and calling this business, I wasn't going to hand over the last pound.

"What do you mean by reimbursement?"

She tapped her ashes into a side plate already filled with butts. "Let's say, double the market value of what you've already sold. And the missing pound."

I guffawed. With two ounces on the table, the money I'd slipped into our till, bills I'd quietly paid for my parents, some clothes I'd gotten for myself, plus the money I'd paid out for the debt, I had nothing left.

"That's unreasonable. I've just delivered fifty-six bags. That should be deducted."

She punched into a calculator. "My sentimentality will be my downfall. As your auntie, I will deduct this delivery. You cannot blab this to the world. People will think I am soft. But you still owe more than ten thousand. Let's round that down to an even ten. The alternative would be very unpleasant."

She handed me the calculator.

"I'll need some time."

"Of course." She bit into an egg roll. "Ho sik wa. These are good." She gestured for Leo and Buddha Boy to grab one. They quickly devoured theirs.

"Ho sik," Leo smacked his lips and reached for another.

"You have twenty-four hours to give me the ten thousand." She took another bite. "These are exceptional, what's in them?"

I gasped—a day? She was giving me a day. That was impossible. I had to soften her up.

"I can share the secret recipe because you are family. But I need three days."

Auntie chuckled.

"Your mother is skilled. At cooking, anyway."

The others all nodded in agreement.

"Johnny, it doesn't matter. I can give you twenty-four hours, seven days, or seven weeks. You won't be able to get me the money."

She was right.

"The only way is to give me the Red Pagoda."

So that's what she wanted. I should have guessed. "It's not mine to give."

"Yes, but you're very persuasive. Your mother owes me money. All I have to do is call it in, she's finished anyway. Twenty-four hours. This is a courtesy on my part."

"Mama owes the Association, not a bunch of gangsters."

Buddha Boy stepped up to me and raised a backhand, but Leo intervened, causing a brief stare-down between them.

Auntie stopped chewing. "Stop." She gave me the hairy eyeball. She'd never been scary like this with me before. "The terms have changed. Any debt owed now comes to me."

Why would she do this to us? I wanted to bust out of there and out of town, hop on a bus to anywhere. I could do that. But she read my mind.

"Don't even think of running, or Golden Boy gets it." She waited. When nothing happened, she exhaled and cursed. "Fat, useless twits." She raised her voice and repeated, "The *Golden Boy*, you stupids."

I heard voices behind a door. It opened. Two of Auntie's men dragged Barry out. I barely recognized him. They'd gagged his mouth. His lips, caked with dried blood, had ballooned. His right eye was swollen. His nose was bent at an off angle.

They removed his gag and let him fall hard to the floor.

"J-Johnny." He coughed.

I froze. I'd never seen anybody beaten up like that. Even though Andrew and Baahir had just had the crap kicked out of them, it was nothing compared to Barry. I crouched and tried to help him up.

"He needs help," I pleaded to Auntie.

"He will get it once you get me what is owed. Until then, we will keep him company. I must say, he is tough. It took days to break him. Be a good boy, twenty-four hours."

Stupid ass, Barry. His loyalty to me almost cost him his life. I had to save him. What a phony Auntie is. All this time, I'd thought she cared about us.

"I trusted you. I thought you were looking out for me." I stepped toward her, but Leo gently shoved me down.

"Don't be a hero," he said.

"Yes, Johnny, don't be like the stupid Golden Boy," Auntie said as she flicked crumbs off her blouse.

"Water, he needs water," I said. "If he dies, this changes everything."

Auntie hesitated, then barked an order. Leo handed me a cup of water, which I helped Barry drink. "Don't worry, man. I'll have you out of here in no time."

"Was this necessary?" I said to Auntie. "He never hurt anybody."

"He hurt my business, Johnny. You know how things work. Now, go, before my generosity and patience are exhausted."

I turned to Barry. "I got you, man. You're going to be okay. I'll get you out of here, I promise."

Buddha Boy escorted me out of the building into the slow, cold rain.

What the hell was I going to do? I had a pound of weed. Barry was still up there, beat up and trapped. He was in real shit, and I was drowning in it. He'd stolen from Auntie, who'd fallen in with the triads, and he'd gotten me into his mess. He'd used me. He'd used my family and our restaurant. I walked around the building toward Grange Park, sidestepping large puddles and almost tripping on the slippery, wet leaves. I sat on a damp bench and gazed at the grey apartment building.

I could sell the remaining pound for cheap real fast. I could stand outside Manny's, probably unload an ounce before the morning bell, drive over to Harbord Collegiate and Central Commerce and do the lunch crowd there. Even at bargain prices, I could easily walk away from all this with a pocket of money.

I don't owe Barry anything. He could've warned me. He should've warned me.

I'm eighteen and have the Vega, even if it sounds ready to die. I could run away.

Auntie would come to the restaurant. Maybe kill Barry. That idiot, he'd almost died saving me when we were children—he didn't run away when we needed him. Does that make me slimier than him?

The park was dark and empty. The rain had stopped after stirring up the musty, earthy smell of decomposing leaves. I decided I didn't need twenty-four hours. I had a plan. I could beat Auntie at her own game and save everybody.

Chapter 41

The Big Bet

I SAT UP and returned to the building as Auntie and her posse left. They saw me approach, stepping through puddles of water in my Kodiaks. Leo shielded her from me. She was holding an umbrella over herself.

"Shouldn't you be getting me money?" she asked.

"I have a better idea. We play one round—four games," I said. "An abbreviated match. You invite Mr. Ho and whoever else, I don't care. Everybody antes ten thousand."

She whistled. "That's a forty thousand-dollar pot. You already owe me $10K. How will you find the buy-in to play?"

"I can offer collateral."

She guffawed. "What do you have that's worth that?"

I bit the inside of my mouth. "Me."

She tilted her head as though she'd missed an important detail.

"I win, I pay you off, you let Barry go, and you stay away from the Red Pagoda. Forever."

"You?" She laughed.

"You can't lose this way."

"Ah, but you're leaving something out," she said. "And when I win?"

I knew she was overconfident.

She twirled her umbrella back and forth like a school-girl playing in the rain.

"You'd get the pot, and you'd get me for the next six months, part-time, because I have to finish school. I move whatever you have to sell. If someone else wins, you cover my losses. I'm still indebted to you."

She stopped twirling her umbrella. "One year, full-time. I'm lending you ten thousand. One year."

"No. I take all the risks. I even pay for my gas. And I still have to finish school. You get free labour and a growing network of customers for six months."

"Johnny, I can take that restaurant from your family now. We both know you won't come up with what belongs to me. What a smart boy. You almost had me. But it's like you said, I can't lose." I imagined Auntie and my family in a dark room under a naked light bulb with her triad goons standing by, where she'd force us to sign over the restaurant.

"Sure, you can muscle us out of the restaurant. You get the cockroaches, the plumbing that always backs up, the food suppliers who always short the count—you get it all. We'd be gone, as would our network of weed customers who trust and know me. You'd have to start from scratch. Besides, hurting a white boy? What are you going to do, kill him? You don't need that attention, even if he is a thief."

She twitched her nose. "One year of you. Forget school. I want you full-time. We may have bigger plans. Then you can keep your shithole restaurant."

That meant three things: I would not graduate from CTS, I'd never be able to get into any college, and lastly, the triads would be all over us. Plus, the risks and chances of getting caught suddenly went up. The restaurant was lucrative both as a restaurant and a drug depot. She wasn't going to let it go, we both knew that. The triads and Auntie would swallow me and my family whole.

Regardless of the terms, I needed to play my way out. I had to grab a seat at her mahjong table. I slowly exhaled, then half bowed in agreement.

"Come tomorrow sap dim—ten o'clock will work. Come earlier, and you can join the beggars for a congee breakfast."

I tried not to wince at that slight.

I haven't yet figured out how to deal with my parents and Mr. Miller. If he goes to the police or my parents, there's no way I'll be delivering again, weed or anything else. But if I win, and I believe I can, we'll be free and clear. Then I can go back to just being a loser or whatever.

Chapter 42

The Paper Family

I TOSSED AND turned all night.

I know I can beat Auntie. Even Mama says I'm good at mahjong and very lucky. Auntie intimidates people, but I'm not scared.

No, that's a lie. I am scared. It's why I couldn't sleep.

"Fear is a normal reaction." Bruce circled the room in attack mode, with fresh scratch marks on his face and chest. He licked his blood. "So long as you can manage it before it becomes uncontrollable anger, raging hate, and needless suffering, it can work for you. An empty mind is impervious to clutter."

"Easy for you to say. You never looked scared. Determined, pissed off, maybe, focused for sure, but never scared. In all your movies, you just crashed in and kicked their asses. End of story."

"There are greater regrets than a beatdown," he said.

"Like what?"

"You look in the mirror and see what might have been." He dropped his pose.

"What regrets are you talking about?"

Before Bruce could answer, Baba trundled into the washroom beside my room and let out a smoker's cough. He cleared his throat into the toilet and peed. Baba would be the first down there.

I hid under the covers and drifted back to sleep until the smell of bacon frying in the kitchen below woke me. In the laneway, the jaws of the garbage truck crushed its debris.

I reviewed mahjong strategies in my head. Auntie liked to start by winning small hands to build up to a winning streak, blocking off the big hand she usually built toward.

I could honestly tell Mr. Miller I was done dealing drugs. And maybe have another chance at Angie. She could help find girlfriends for Andrew and Baahir. That would patch things up between us. Then we could go on dates to the Eaton Centre, roller skating, and maybe even Swiss Chalet.

My bedroom trembled as the College streetcar rumbled. Mama entered the room without knocking like she always did, despite my complaints. Once, when I was flipping through one of Andrew's *Playboys*, she walked in. She was more startled than me, but she pretended not to notice and left. At least this time, she brought a big bowl of my favourite soup.

"Why are you not at school?"

"Morning spares."

She cocked an eye. We both knew I was lying. I pulled a deflection play, one I don't think she saw coming. "What's the deal with you and Auntie?"

I expected her to automatically deny there was anything wrong between them, but she surprised me. She sat on the bed, smoothed out my comforter, and covered my toes with the blanket. Then she abruptly stood up, walked over to the window, and stared out.

First, she told me stuff I already knew about the two of them growing up in the same village, even though they never really knew one another back then. Auntie is a decade older and immigrated to Canada more than twenty years ago. Four years before Mama.

"Your aunt and uncle sponsored me to come to Canada. They listed me as their daughter. They arranged everything, paying an agent in Hong Kong and one here."

"What? But I thought . . ."

"In the village, all Wongs are family. Only on paper is she my mama. Only in our words is she your aunt. That is why my real mama and baba could never come."

Frig. That she hadn't seen her parents in more than twenty years wasn't something I ever thought about. She rarely spoke about them. Occasionally, she'd get cassette tapes sent from home. She said they were from her family but nothing more. She'd listen to them repeatedly behind closed doors, then emerge with red eyes.

There are times I can't wait to get away from Mama. She must've dreamt the opposite about her mama. I didn't know what to say, but I didn't want the conversation to end. "What was it like living with them, Auntie and Uncle?"

She shook her head ever so slightly. "Ho ma faan. Very frustrating. Your aunt and uncle did not get along. They fought all the time. And I was in the middle, indebted to them, then and always. A difficult debt to repay . . . you have no idea."

"Wait, what else do you owe her? Because I have a plan—"

"M sai nay lay."

"What do you mean it's not important? If she's legally your mama, then Leo's your brother and my uncle? That's pretty weird."

"Only on paper. It means nothing now. The government doesn't care anymore." She explained that not long after I was born, amnesty was granted to illegal Chinese immigrants. Some stepped forward. But many didn't trust the Canadian government and, like her, remained quiet. Nevertheless, she moved out of Auntie's house and then met Baba.

"Was Auntie okay with that?"

She glared at me like I'd uncovered something. "What did she say to you?"

"Nothing. But you and her are always mad about something, so I wonder if it's because you left."

"A vast mist divides us, but it does not concern you." She pointed to the soup. "Eat before it gets cold." Then she headed for the door.

I came close to telling her about the upcoming game, but I'm glad I kept my mouth shut. There's no way I can tell her I've been selling drugs. Instead, I squeezed in another question. "You tell me to stay away, but why do *you* keep returning?"

"Ah ma deok lo."

There has to be more to her conflict with Auntie than just playing mahjong, but she was out the door before I could ask her anything more.

Chapter 43

Three Fingers

I slurped my breakfast down in minutes. It was exactly what I needed, as it made my body forget I'd spent most of the night contemplating the upcoming game. Bruce always said, "As you think, so shall you become." I thought I could take her down. No, I *knew* I could. I scribbled a saying on the chalkboard:

> *Courage is not the absence of fear. He who does not eat Chinese food will accomplish nothing in life.*

The first line was Bruce's, and the second riffed off a Muhammad Ali quote.

Bruce nodded his approval. "But what would Johnny Wong say?"

I hesitated before wiping the board clean, then wrote:

> *I accept the challenge and embrace the fear.*
> *There can be no failure in eating Chinese food.*
> —J. Wong

The morning was auspiciously bright, and my adrenaline was pumping, so I walked to the Wong Association instead of driving.

Leo greeted me at the door, wearing a bowling shirt. This time, he was Chester. "It's going to be weird having you around for the next year," he said.

If he was trying to psych me out, it didn't work. Instead, I laughed. "Dream on, Leo. I rule. I've outplayed my mama many times."

He broke into a non-evil smile, like he was rooting for me. But the smile dropped, and he looked around before lowering his voice. "Johnny, you can't beat her, but you can still walk. Get lost. It's not too late. Go now."

I stared at him, unable to tell if he was trying to fake me out or if he had my back. What did he know?

Mr. Ho came up behind me. "Johnny, are you ready for the big game? One of us will take your auntie down." He and Leo exchanged nods.

"It's going to be me," I said.

Leo opened the door and ushered me in.

The community room was quiet. A couple of uncles saw me make a beeline toward the stairs. Uncle Kwong must have sensed a big game. He shuffled my way and wished me luck. For the first time, I felt like a warrior. I climbed the creaky stairs, each step louder than the one before.

Auntie stood atop the stairs. The backlight highlighted her silhouette. She said nothing at first, just sipped her cup of tea. "You have what belongs to me?"

I nodded, then gave her the small bundle in my backpack—the remaining pound of weed. "Where's Barry?"

She led me to the storage room where Barry sat, half slumped.

Through a freshly bleeding lip, he muttered. "Everything's groovy, man. Just win this stupid domino game."

In the gaming room, Mr. Ho introduced me to Char Lai. I'd seen him around Chinatown. He was the owner of the Imperial, Chinatown's newest and biggest white-tablecloth restaurant. Auntie had told him my parents ran the Red Pagoda. He snickered at me like I was a village rat.

Auntie reminded us of the house rules and the $10K ante. In one round of four games, whoever scored the most after four rounds would take $25K, second place would get $10K, third place—$5K, and last place—zero.

We drew seats: Mr. Ho drew East to start the game, Auntie landed South, Char Lai, West, and me, the North. We stacked the tiles and built the wall. I arranged mine with ninja-like precision.

I was dealt great tiles, needing only a few to complete three pungs (three of a kind), a hand that thwarted other players by taking tiles out of play. I tried to set a fast pace, picking up and discarding before anyone knew what was happening with my hand. Dragons and winds! Take that, *suckas*! Luck was running my way.

Auntie bit into her lip, something I've rarely seen her do. She must have been stunned to see me win the first game so handily. *Hahaha!* She gave Mr. Ho a nasty look and threw one my way before retreating behind her visor. Char Lai scowled, then swore—something about wishing my whole family would die.

The second game was slower. They kept glancing at each other and re-examining their hands and the table before discarding. I had very little at first, but a couple of solid draws put me in line for a semi-pure hand of the bamboo suit with some honour tiles. A decent hand, I figured. My heart was pumping fast. Things were lining up for me. I tried to play it cool behind my concealed wall. I waited and waited, drawing crap tiles I promptly threw back in. Finally, Auntie dropped a 1 Bamboo, carved as a bird. That made me think of Bruce, flipping the bird to Hollywood.

"Sik wu." I reached for the bird, holding back a fist pump as I laid out my three winning bamboo combos and remaining honour tiles. Mr. Ho and Char Lai folded their tiles down without a word. I had a solid lead. I'd won the first two games. I wanted to go get Barry and tell him we were going home. I was going to tell Mama that I'd cleared her debts, that I'd saved Barry, and that I'd beaten Auntie—with thousands of dollars to show for it. I'd buy a decent set of wheels, and maybe Angie would come to the drive-in with me, the one past the airport at Highway 7 and 27.

We reshuffled the bone, ivory, and bamboo tiles. More than ever, they sounded like music. I imagined a Chinese opera done in disco style, the sounds of mahjong tiles in the background, a line of sword-wielding Laoshengs dancing behind the Qingyi.

The third game started cautiously. Auntie tapped her left index finger on the table twice. Then, her right index twitched. Was that seven times or six? Mr. Ho cleared his throat. After several discards that drew no interest, he dropped a 7 Bamboo, exactly what I needed to convert my pair into a three of a kind.

"Pung," I shouted.

"Sik wu," Auntie rebutted, gleefully overriding me. She snatched the discard. She revealed the remainder of her winning hand: all bamboos.

Shit. I stared at her winning combo—a pure hand, one of the most coveted wins. My lead had shrunk. But she still had to win the fourth game and win it big. As long as she didn't do that, I'd still have enough points to win first place and twenty-five thousand dollars.

The tiles felt cold as we readied for the final game. Usually, we could hear the uncles' laughter and their shuffling tiles below. But all the sounds outside our game room had stopped. Mr. Ho ground his teeth. Auntie sucked on her cigarette.

She had a few good pickups, then dropped a run. I didn't start with much but played for a ping wu—a quick, easy win with the most basic mishmash of suits, but all runs. My victory seemed assured.

Auntie discarded everything except characters, which signalled to everyone which suit she was collecting.

Her right index finger twitched—twice. Mr. Ho foolishly dropped a 2 Character, which Auntie picked up. She revealed a run of 1-2-3.

Mr. Ho giving her that 2 Character was a total amateur move. Too coincidental. I studied Mr. Ho's face and watched her hands. Were they signalling to each other?

Char Lai, having drawn and discarded, was waiting for me. He nudged me. "Hey, it's your turn."

I wanted to ask him if he'd seen what I'd seen, but what would I do? Call them out?

"Are you playing or what?" Mr. Ho said.

I tried to refocus. She needed to win a semi-pure hand to tie me. I could still walk out with Barry, and our debt would be cleared. But I couldn't see Auntie playing for a tie. She was going for something bigger—another pure hand, possibly of all runs, for an even bigger score with enough points to catch me.

My shirt was sticking to my skin as I scanned the other players. Why wasn't there a window in this room? What if I lost? *No, think positive.* I still had a huge lead. I reminded myself that Bruce never panicked.

I picked up a 2 Circle, completing a run behind my wall. Things were looking good, but I tried not to let on. I already had a pair. I was two easy runs from the win.

Char Lai called a pung on my discard, resetting my turn. I was happy to give him that. If he won, I won. I drew another tile to complete another run. Anyone's discard could complete my final run. I held my breath and waited.

Mr. Ho picked up and then glanced at Auntie's twitchy fingers. Goddammit it, for sure, they were communicating. He dropped a 5 Character. No! What an idiot. Everybody knew she was collecting characters. Why would he do that?

She shouted as she snatched the discard, "Sik wu!" Then she unveiled her hand. It was as I feared—all characters, all runs. She'd maxed out the score on a pure hand, sixty-four points. Her iron face dissolved into a shy schoolgirl's smile, as though someone had just asked her to dance. She'd destroyed us.

"That's bullshit," I said to Mr. Ho. "You knew what she needed. You let her have it."

"Johnny, you can't talk to him like that," Auntie said.

Char Lai also joined in and swore at Mr. Ho for his supremely idiotic move and for throwing the game.

"No way, you guys ..." I looked at Auntie and Mr. Ho. "You guys ..." I couldn't outright call them cheats. I slammed my hand on the table. Tiles jumped into the air.

Auntie gasped. "Johnny, mind yourself. Be a man. You lost fair and square."

I dropped my head into my open hands and closed my eyes, wishing to wake up in the cocoon of my comforter to find out this was an elaborate nightmare. Leo clapped, quickly squashing my hopes. Mr. Ho and Char Lai muttered curses. He and Mr. Ho handed over small bundles of bills wrapped in elastic bands. Auntie promptly counted them and merged them into a big roll of bills. She smiled, and they left, quietly dejected. She ordered Leo to get her a snack on Dundas.

That left us alone in the room. I peeked through my fingers. It was just her and me and the forty thousand dollars on the table. I could snatch it and be out the door real fast. After all, it was mine. I should have won. She tried to light a cigarette but dropped the lighter. She bent down and fumbled under the dark table. I saw my chance and lurched forward to grab the money. Leo grabbed my shoulder from behind and threw me back into place.

"What are you doing here? Where's my snack?" Auntie said to Leo before lighting her cigarette.

"Lo bak goh, okay?" Leo asked her.

"I don't want peasant food. This is a celebratory meal. Get me some roast squab." She stuffed the roll of bills into her waist bag and dismissed Leo.

"We have both won, Johnny." She exhaled her smoke.

I slumped into my seat.

"You still have your restaurant. You still get to deliver. I insist. It is business as usual. But you will have a reliable supply with a bigger customer base. You will have professional managerial support. You may need to hire another driver, though, not Stanley. He scratched up my new Buick last week parking. Useless boy. I'll find someone."

She leaned forward. "You were always a good player for a boy. I taught you, remember?"

Her face hadn't changed, yet she appeared unrecognizable.

"This is a man's game. You can learn good business skills. Make serious money. Based on your model, we will open several restaurants. I have partners who will want to meet you. They will have even higher expectations than I do. You would not want to disappoint them."

I gulped and thought of the restaurant that was blown up.

"I will have you manage them. Wouldn't that be marvellous?" She chuckled.

She had me in a tightening noose.

"A year, a whole year," I whispered.

"Maybe more, maybe you like it. It's not like you're going to college."

I winced. But was she wrong? I looked straight into her cheating eyes and wanted to puke. What a fool I've been. I wanted to believe family meant more than money, that she had my back. But she had sucked me into her triad underworld of loan sharks and cheating. Working for Mama and Baba sucked, but I was needed and never felt played. Auntie would find a way to keep me when my year was up. There would be no college for me. The closest I'd get would be delivering dope to college students who actually have a future.

"It was foolish to dream. Some things are inevitable," Auntie said.

Mr. Miller's idea of me getting away, becoming a writer, and watching Dave Keon play hockey have become a cruel joke. Maybe it's been a cruel joke all along. It was never going to happen. She was right. I didn't have anything else.

"My vice principal knows about the weed delivery service. He's going to tell my parents."

She paused and rolled her lighter in her knuckles. "Let him. Your parents will be outraged. They will yell, scream, and assure this vice principal that your delivery days are over. And they will be, for a while. We'll get someone else. You will open other restaurants, like I said."

"Barry measures and bags and does the marketing side of things. I need him," I said, lying.

"Your Golden Boy broke into our basement and stole from me what you've been selling. I will not forgive that."

"What do you mean? Are you going to ... to kill him?" My fists clenched.

Auntie chuckled. "You've been watching the *Godfather* movies. We are not Italian."

My shoulders sagged with relief.

"No, Johnny, the Golden Boy lives. But he will never steal again. He will be an example for all. Three of his fingers. We take those, then we are even."

Leo shot his mother a disbelieving look and whispered, "Are you sure, Mama?"

"This is what is wrong with the world today. Men have become wimps." She shook her head at Leo and me.

"Yes, Leo, we can, and we will. Unless ..." She raised an eyebrow at me. "Unless you do it for us? Prove to me your loyalty. You chop one off instead of three. It has to be you. We will call it a workplace accident. That should satisfy my partners. Leo will supervise and bring me back his finger. As a gesture of good faith, I will let you decide which finger. You save two fingers this way. You are the hero again. Johnny to the rescue—ho yeh, ho yeh." She mocked and applauded.

I hung my head. There was no way I could take anybody's finger off.

"Go home, Johnny, and forget about school. Take the rest of the afternoon off. Stanley and Leo will bring Barry to you tonight. Ngo ho hoi sam. You should be happy, too." She beamed. "Now go."

Chapter 44

Fallen Heroes, False Gods

I SAT IN my car in the laneway between Henry and McCaul streets. The garage where the fire that nearly killed us is gone now. There's just crushed rock in its place. I pulled the joint out of my wallet, the first one Barry gave me at his place more than a month ago.

I sparked it up with the car lighter.

When I sucked the weed smoke in, my chest exploded with flames. I tried to spit it out but coughed hard and dry until my throat felt like it had been sanded down. Once I stopped coughing, I thought of tossing the weed, not wanting my raw throat to go through another burn. But part of me wanted the hurt. I relit the joint and hardly inhaled. It didn't matter. My insides still smouldered. I ground the joint beneath my Kodiak.

I don't remember how I wound up on Yonge Street. I dodged a small crowd protesting in front of a massage parlour. They wanted all such businesses shut down. Several protestors carried Bibles.

If I were killed, would Mama get that worked up and vocal? Would she take charge, protest, and demand action? I can't picture her doing that.

I could rat out Auntie to the police and save Barry. Mama and Baba might be able to hold onto the restaurant. Why should they be punished? They weren't involved. Except Jane's already in trouble with the cops, who might think it's a family operation. Plus, if the rumours about the triads having bought their way into the police were true, I'd be dead meat before dinner. Even if those rumours weren't true, the police worked for the Man, and the Man constantly screwed the Chinese. The uncles were right not to have any faith in the authorities.

I drove to Kensington Market, parked, and bought a few patties and a ginger beer at the Jamaican patty place. I sat on a bench in front of Sasmart, by the tiny park. A homeless man occupied a patch of grass beside me. I shared my patties with him and threw a few crumbs for the pigeons, who seemed disappointed with my count.

I considered heading to Andrew's with a patty and another ginger beer as a peace offering, but I knew he didn't want anything to do with me. I'd blown that. Heck, even Baahir had moved on.

Baba took off when things were tough. What if we all did that together? We could close the restaurant and hop on a bus. I heard there were more Chinese in Vancouver than here. We could blend in. No one would find us. Or maybe it'd be safer for us to split up, plus Jane would drive me crazy on a long trip. Mama could go wherever her daydreams take her, Baba and Jane could return to Vancouver. I'd find someplace to rot.

Would they really chop Barry's fingers off? If I call their bluff, it might cost him three fingers.

I hadn't figured out what to say to my parents, but I didn't want to be alone and I knew I had to go home. They would blame me for Jane's drug charge. They'd freak out once Mr. Miller showed up at the restaurant, which would be any minute now. Maybe with the police. My parents would go ballistic. They'd blame me.

"Don't think, just do," Bruce had said. "Have faith in yourself."

Well, that was garbage. I had believed in myself and gotten my ass kicked in the most significant way possible. I realized I couldn't trust some stupid kung fu God.

"Calm down, Johnny," Bruce said, wearing his yellow jumpsuit with the black stripes as he knelt atop a mailbox splattered with pigeon shit.

I scattered more crumbs, leading to a dust-up between two pigeons, which made the homeless man chuckle. He flashed a toothless grin, which reminded me of Uncle Kwong. I offered the man the last of my ginger beer, which he accepted.

"Calm down?" I said to Bruce. "I just blew my life up."

"In great attempts, it is glorious even to fail."

"Great, hit me with another useless Confucius saying."

"It is Taoist, not Confucianist. You know that."

"It's all the same fortune cookie crap. Did you feel glorious dying in your mistress's apartment?"

His cocky grin evaporated.

I laughed. "Here we are, two losers. Even Jane and Mr. Miller tried to tell me you weren't all that."

"You know how I like to think of myself?" Bruce said as he glanced at the homeless man stretching out on the grass. "I was a human being, which is to be open to learning from everything, even things we don't want."

"Calling it a learning opportunity is a pathetic consolation prize. You—the kung fu God—screwed up, just like I did."

"You don't mean that, Johnny. You are still learning to bring out the best in yourself and . . ."

"—fulfill my potential. Right? Shut up. Just shut up, leave me alone, and get out of my head, you phony loser. Do you know what you are? You're an inventor. You invented another kind of caricature. One who beats people up in the movies while spitting out Chinese proverbs. It's an impossible trail you've blazed. I could do a thousand push-ups, and I'd never be you. You've cursed us all."

"Be calm, my friend." He shook his head. "This moment is a chance to expand. Slow it down, be one with it, bend if that is where it takes you."

"Do you think any of that will help the kids you left behind? Do you know what it's like when a parent checks out on their kid?"

Bruce blinked.

"Do you think Linda told your kids that their daddy dropping dead was a learning opportunity for them?"

He rose from his kneeling position, his chest heaving. He towered atop the mailbox, looking ready to drop-kick into me. His temper was legendary. He used to run the streets of Hong Kong with the threat of his fists. Hong Kong newspapers said he'd once pulled a knife on a director.

He pointed at me.

I braced myself.

His fists tightened, but his eyes moistened, and a single tear trickled toward his mouth. He licked it, then mouthed two names, Brandon and Shannon—his children. He did a backflip and disappeared.

Chapter 45

In Synch

SEEING BRUCE LIKE that cratered my insides. I'd been mean, cruel even. He'd always talked about me being me. He'd never actually said I had to be him. The person putting an impossible standard on myself was me.

I had to face my family. But I also had to fix things. The restaurant's lunch shift was ending when I walked in. There were still some straggler tables. All but one had bills set down amid fortune cookie wrappers and little white fortunes.

"If you're going to skip school, you could've helped out over lunch," Jane said. "We were busy."

"Shut up, Jane!"

Mama came out with a tray of coffee cups to shelve and saw me. She bit her lip. I think she'd heard what I'd said to Jane. She looked disappointed in me.

She pointed to the "living room"—table eleven—for me to sit down. We were going to talk. We never have family meetings with customers around. Instead, we yell in the kitchen or drown in unspoken words. I wanted to hide, confess everything, and beg for forgiveness like a child. She'd make it all better.

She sat with a cup of black coffee. "What do you have to say?" she said in Toisanese.

I shrugged, a reflex built on years of emotional distance, forgetting my option to tell her to start packing and get out of town.

She leaned into me. "Why were you at Auntie's instead of school?" How did she know I was at the Association? An icky heaviness like sweet-and-sour sauce enveloped me. "How much did you lose?" she asked casually, as though I'd dropped an order slip on the floor.

"Faan see." Everything. I lowered my head, as though I were five and had gotten caught doing something idiotic, like shaving. "I'm sorry, Mama."

I wanted her to say it would all be okay, that we all make mistakes and that my heart was in the right place. But she's not that kind of mother.

Her head shifted as though she couldn't bear to look at me. She lit a cigarette. "What is 'everything'?"

"Everything for the next year. She wants to get into the restaurant and special-delivery business. She wants me to manage things. In exchange, your loan is paid off, and you get to keep the restaurant. Barry will be set free, more or less, minus a finger."

"What do you mean, special-delivery business?"

I exhaled and looked away. "Drugs," I said, still in Toisanese. "But remember, the restaurant is free and clear now."

She covered her eyes with the palms of her hands, then took a heavy drag of her cigarette. "Johnny, how could you be so careless? She trapped you, too."

"You owed her five thousand dollars, and Auntie said the uncles on the executive were pressuring her to call in big debts like yours. They were going to take the restaurant."

She shook her head. "Is that what she told you? The uncles? They're more interested in planting a garden. Don't believe everything she says. I would have paid the debt back. Your Auntie runs the games and the loans now. She pays for protection. But she's always had bigger ideas to make money. I'm not surprised she's partnered with the triads. Or that she's selling drugs."

I paused. "You knew about Auntie all along?"

She shrugged. "There were good reasons I told you to keep some distance, but you were very fond of her, and she of you."

"Well, it's too late now. I have to continue drug-running for her out of the restaurant and help her with whatever expansion plans she has. Mr. Miller already busted me, but Auntie says you can help get around that." As I spoke, it sunk in how much I'd sucked my family into *my* mess.

She banged her forehead with a closed fist. She seemed madder at herself than at me.

"Mama?" I sounded like a frightened little kid. "There's something else."

"Mut yeh— What? About Barry?"

I nodded. "I have to chop his finger off. Otherwise, Auntie will take three." I explained Barry's role in the whole fiasco.

She gasped. "She has gone too far. Do you know what you've gotten into?" Instead of lecturing or screaming at me, she just shook her head.

Baba came over and asked why we were sitting around when there was work to be done.

I told him everything. Mama looked away when I mentioned her debt. Then I told them about Auntie's goons pounding the crap out of Barry and threatening to do worse. Finally, I told them about the game I'd lost and what it meant for us.

To Baba's credit, he didn't lose it, at least not right away.

Mama dropped her forehead into the palms of her hands. "Then the restaurant is under her control, and you are locked in with her. As for Barry's finger, she is dramatic. She would mutilate a gwai lo? So unnecessary."

By then, Jane had eagerly joined in. The three of them stood around the table, facing me. A customer broke our silence, asking for more coffee, which I gladly got up to pour before returning. Mama gently tapped her fingers as she stared off.

"I had her beat," I said.

"What?" Baba said.

"I have a plan," I whispered.

"Boy, have you screwed up. You think we still trust you with a plan?" Jane started to laugh and shook her head. "Suddenly, my three dime bags at school don't look like such a big deal."

"Shut up." Mama folded her arms and glared at her. "You knew about this?"

"Don't tell her to shut up," Baba said, raising his voice. "She is just following his footsteps. Her dai goh set a horrible example."

"No, wait a minute, he didn't make or tell me to do anything," Jane said.

Suddenly, I felt like I had a sister who cared about me. But it didn't last.

"I had nothing to do with it," she said. "If we get into trouble, it's his fault."

"Shh, stop it, Jane." Baba struggled to lower his voice. "We could *all* go to jail," he said in Toisanese.

Baba blamed Mama for not staying away from Auntie and borrowing from the Association in the first place. He blamed me for getting involved with Auntie. They went around in circles, but Mama never dumped on me. Instead, she said the current loan was her business and hers alone.

"You took out a loan without telling me." Baba shook his head.

"I just said it's *my* business."

Baba blasted Mama and me. She quietly defended me, taking hits from Baba when she could have easily piled on.

"I have a plan," I said again.

They stopped arguing.

"Let's just burn their building down," Jane said, missing the irony, given her history with matches. Or was she serious?

"No, of course not." I took a deep breath. "Auntie won, but she's beatable. I had her. I know she cheated. And I think she does that a lot."

Mama glanced at me, pulled up a chair and sat beside me. "What have you seen?"

I explained how Auntie and Mr. Ho cheated together. I re-enacted the game for her.

"She taps and twitches her fingers. It's hardly noticeable. From what I could see, I'm guessing each finger on her left hand corresponds to the suit she needs, and then the taps on her right hand to show how many she needs. She also—"

"Gently scratches her neck and cheek," Mama said. "She's a very skilled player, but I've wondered how she elevated her game in the past few months."

"So what?" Baba said. "You still lost to a gangster. It's not like you can get your money back."

"No, Baba, but she's beatable in a fair game. I think I can do it."

Baba shook his head. "It doesn't matter, it's too late. You screwed your life—mo yung doi. It's over." Baba calling me useless was different than Mama saying it. There was anger behind the words.

"What a witch," Jane said. "There's no such thing as a fair game with her."

"There could be." I looked at Mama. "Let me take her on, one on one, in a two-person game." It was how Mama had taught me, and how Auntie had schooled her. It was lightning fast, unlike the traditional style. Few people played it. It would be hard to keep up with her, but in a straight game, I believed I could.

"What are you talking about?" Baba almost screamed. "Play her? With what? So you could lose again?"

I hadn't thought through what I had to gamble with. "I could offer another year."

"It is a two-person mahjong game with double-trouble rules," Mama whispered. "It is brilliant, but I won't allow it."

"Why not?" I asked.

"Because there is no incentive for her. You are already indebted to her. She likely believes you won't be able to leave after a year, anyway. Except ..."

"Except what?"

Mama exhaled. "Me."

"What do you mean?"

"It should be me who plays her," she said, sighing. "We cannot stand by as you throw your life away. I am your mama. I will always worry and feel responsible for you, especially now that you are out of your depth. No, it is me who should take on your auntie. You don't understand how this is my burden."

I protested, saying how I'd gotten us into this, that it was on me to get us out. We disagreed. I could see she had made her mind up. And for the first time in a long time, I didn't cringe or get all twisted up about it. Letting her take over was like exhaling after holding my breath for so long.

Mama had once put together thirteen orphans. She could beat her. Maybe it was beyond me. It wasn't on me to hold the family together anymore. It never should have been.

I nodded, but barely, and she did likewise. We were in synch, like a two-person opera where she was the Qingyi, the most crucial character—dignified, serious, decent—and I was the fiddler.

"Did you not hear me?" Baba said, interrupting our moment. "Johnny screwed up by agreeing to allow the triads' drugs into our restaurant. We have nothing to play with. Our car, our restaurant, what does she not have already?"

"I can work for her for three years," Mama said. "I am sure she will use me like a servant girl once again. It's me she wants. She'll ruin Johnny to get to me. We cannot allow him to be a drug dealer and her whipping boy."

"What choice do we have? He screwed up. He's a man, and he must live with it, not us. He has to work for her, not us."

I was about to get up and leave, but I sensed something in Mama.

"If Johnny has to deliver through our restaurant, it is our problem, too," she said. "If I lose, I can offer her three years of my life and the restaurant. She would love the chance to degrade me every day. Nothing would give her more satisfaction. If I win, she leaves us alone. Perhaps I can finally walk away. Johnny leaves town, away from this."

Baba lowered his voice but seethed with a hiss, which was way worse than shouting. "I won't have anything to do with it. Besides, she will never release you. You won't do this to my restaurant."

My restaurant. Of all the times I'd felt forgotten or ignored, this was worse. The restaurant mattered more to him than I did. It stung, and it made me want to run away first before he did it to me again.

But Mama ignored Baba.

She calmly untied her apron, left it behind the counter, and told us to stay put. She adjusted her hair and grabbed her cigarettes.

"Where are you going? We have a restaurant to run," Baba said. "The phone's ringing. We have orders."

"Have you not been listening? It's our restaurant in name only unless we do something."

"This is stupid. You're being stupid," Baba said, pointing at her, but she'd already tuned him out. His nostrils flared at me, and he breathed fire, ready to charge. Seeing your father about to lose it on you, even when you're a man yourself, makes you a kid again. Not the kid throwing a ball back and forth with your old man, but the kid who climbed the tree to impress him then couldn't get down.

I turned to Mama. "I'm coming with you." It was more of a statement than a request.

Baba stormed off, but not before he looked at me with disgust.

She didn't say no, so I got myself ready, although there wasn't much for me to do—no lightsaber to grab, no X-wing to power up, no crunches or push-ups to do. Just my mama to follow.

Chapter 46

Jane's In Charge

"I want to come," Jane said without any trace of her usual smart-aleck tone or rolling eyes. "It's my life, too."

She was right. We were playing with her future, as well.

"No, I need you here. You're the only one we can trust to look after things," Mama said.

That was as big as any hug for Jane, who nodded.

Just as we were about to leave, two CTS boys in Adidas shirts entered. I recognized them as hot rodders who liked to burn rubber up and down Harbord Street, cruising to nearby high schools for girls. They stomped their cigarettes onto the floor and sat at a table. "I want me some hot and spicy Chinese meat."

In Toisanese, Jane said, "I know those guys," and grabbed a broom for their butts and ashes.

She bent over to sweep when one of the boys stood and grabbed her behind.

Jane sprang up with a shriek. Her eyes burned with fear and rage. Before Mama or I could react, she smacked the boy's ankles with the broom, sending him hard onto the floor and howling in pain.

"Stupid bitch," the boy on the floor cried out.

"What did you call me?" Jane's chest heaved. "Get out of my restaurant, now." She shook with eyes widened.

The boy yelped and floundered on his back like a fish out of water, grabbing his ankle.

She stared down the other boy who had risen from his seat. He raised his palms and drew back in meek surrender.

"You're in my house now." Jane clutched the broom handle like a baseball bat. "Don't you dare touch me or anybody like that again."

She tracked the boys with a deadly stare as they dragged themselves out.

Mama and I looked at one another, then at Jane.

Jane's breathing slowed, and she loosened her grip on the broom handle. "What? I was just showing some 'emotional content'."

Mama smiled at Jane. "Don't hurt anybody, leng nui. You have a family restaurant to run."

Mama had never called Jane "pretty daughter" before. It had always just been "Jane," and rarely with a smile. Jane beamed, projecting the same smug confidence she had when addressing a math problem or stealing an eyeliner pencil. Until that moment, I just thought she was annoying. But I realized she had this.

Mama was waiting in the Vega. I jumped in. It coughed and sputtered before stalling completely. I tried it again, and the same thing happened. We exchanged looks. This was not a good sign. I banged the steering wheel and swore.

"We walk." She opened her door, and we got out.

I kicked the bumper and swore at the car.

Then, a welcome, familiar voice said, "Pop your hood. Let me take a look." It was Andrew.

"What are you doing here?" I asked.

"I saw you in class like you were about to cry. I was done giving you the cold shoulder. Then you skipped this morning. I was worried, so I came to check on you, man. Pop your hood. Let's take a look."

At that moment, I could've gift-wrapped him all my Bruce Lee posters. He poked around the engine while I looked at my watch. Mama stood by patiently, chain-smoking. Andrew asked me a few questions. "Sounds like you need a new fuel filter. I can get my dad to drop one off real quick, although you've been a real jerk lately, so I should say: 'Screw you'."

His presence already told me we were good, but he was right.

"I wouldn't blame you for telling me off. I was a jerk. I'm sorry, man."

"Okay, screw you. You want a new filter or what?"

I nodded and smiled.

"Can you wait, or do you need to go somewhere?"

"We need to go now," Mama said.

Andrew handed me the keys to his Pinto in the laneway. "I'll call my dad and get you a new filter. I might even clean out your carb. We'll get your shitbox going by the time you get back. Then you can tell me why you've been such a stupid shit."

"Have I got a story for you." I jingled his keys. "You're sure we can borrow this?"

He nodded. "Just don't leave my radio on some disco station. Now, get out of here."

Chapter 47

The Big Reveal

I TURNED THE key in his ignition, and Rush's new album blasted us. It was hard to think with the music, so I popped the cassette out and turned onto College Street.

Things were starting to sink in. Not too long ago, I'd thought of Auntie as someone who had my back. She had been kind and generous. But there was more to her than I wanted to see. And it made me wonder about Bruce. I'd been fixating only on what made him a legend. There had to be other parts to him. The way he teared up at the sound of his kids' names told me he wasn't like my baba, an emotional vault focused only on making money. Would I want to hear the truth? What if I did and didn't like it? Would I see him any differently?

I turned south onto Spadina and hit a wall of traffic. I wanted to know more about Mama and Auntie. I felt she was taking on Auntie for me and herself, and I wanted to know why.

"What's really going on with you and Auntie? You said she wanted to get back at you."

I rolled the window down a bit. The damp late-November cold filled the car.

"Ngon yel." Always *it doesn't matter*. But this time, it mattered, and I wouldn't let her brush me off.

"I want to know. Or I stop the car. Now."

She stared out the window and said nothing.

Finally, she said, "No, keep driving." After a long, slow breath, she spoke in Toisanese. She said that when she first arrived in Canada, Auntie had been kind to her. "She was married, but I think she was lonely. There were very few Chinese women then. She and Uncle rarely spoke. But she wanted a servant, not female companionship. Not a sister." She took a heavy drag before flicking her butt out the window.

"Paper daughters were cheaper than sons. So your auntie and uncle, who had Canadian citizenship, found me through the village. They paid a middleman to create documents saying I was their daughter. The middleman arranged for me to come. I still remember those long hours practising answers to the government's questions to trap us. Many gwai lo correctly suspected us. It was, for many, our only option. Their laws did not restrict Europeans in this way. Judging by the gwai lo's disdain for us, you would think the Chinese were the only ones ever to seek a better life."

I thought of Rollie, Mama's gwai lo boyfriend from when I was a kid. Baba was in Vancouver when Rollie, along with the tens of thousands of Americans, evaded the Vietnam War by crossing into Canada. The draft evaders had been welcomed, not met with marches and slogans accusing them of being a threat to the Canadian way of life.

"Auntie and Uncle ran a laundry business inherited from his baba. They worked every day, from early morning to late at night. They made me do the same. I expected to work hard. It is all I have ever known. It is the price of freedom. But here, without my real family, loneliness drained any hope and joy away.

"The laundry was much harder than running our restaurant now. The life of a laundryman was very dull. I spent all my time washing. They had a wooden washing machine that broke down so many times that I had to wash by hand, then iron, press, pack, and deliver clothes. When I wasn't doing laundry, I cooked, cleaned, and shopped for them. They paid me with food, clothing, and a room near the boiler. This was to be my life until they released me from my sponsorship debt.

"We undercut all our competitors, some of whom were once friends of Auntie and Uncle's. We never knew if the government would shut us down or if business would go bad. I know they saved every penny, ready for either a calamity or an opportunity.

"I quickly realized the tension wasn't just work worries. They'd been unable to have a child. She was already thirty.

"One day, while Auntie was out, Uncle and I were manning the laundry. He brought me a red-bean bun from Chinatown. I had not tasted anything so delicious since I left home.

"Days later, Uncle brought egg custard tarts, one for me and one for him. We devoured the goodies but also chit-chatted. He understood that I was lonely, and he said he appreciated my work. He told me he hoped to one day sell the laundry business and open a restaurant. He hoped I would be part of it.

"The treats kept coming, and our talks continued. Always while Auntie was busy. I wasn't clueless. I knew where things were going. Yet I was also happy for any morsel of kindness and attention. It wasn't long before things happened the way he wanted them to.

"I was a nobody. I met your baba after I discovered I was pregnant. Back then, your baba was kind. He did care. It didn't matter to him that I carried your uncle's child. He offered to run off with me and my unborn child. But your auntie discovered our plan and threatened to debase me and my family back in Toisan. She offered a deal: my child for my freedom."

"What?" I shouted out. "Uncle's my real dad?" That explained why Baba had left me, why he's such an ass to me sometimes.

Mama bit her lip and shook her head. "No, listen to me. I was desperate to escape her and marry Baba, but also fearful she would expose me to the government. I was too young and scared to call her bluff, not realizing such exposure could hurt her.

"Your auntie said we could all live in the house and that she would help your baba and I set up our own business with a small loan, that I would be like a live-in aunt so I'd see my child always. But we would have to swear to a lifetime of secrecy."

"No one ever said anything to me about that," I said.

"Of course not. Because it never happened. Living with her would've been unbearable. In the end, I agreed to most of her terms. She pretended she was pregnant while I hid my pregnancy. When my baby was born, the baby had a cleft palate.

"Your aunt was furious, saw that as a bad omen, and threatened to back out of our deal. She laid so much shame on me that I wanted to drown myself. At first, I was so happy to break the deal, but she demanded I continue to work for them. I did not want my child to believe I was nothing but a servant.

"I demanded my freedom. The government was offering amnesty to all paper sons and daughters. All we had to do was tell the truth, and we could stay legally. The threat of deportation would be gone. But we could not trust the government, and I did not step forward like most. I didn't tell your auntie that. I didn't want her to think she could get me deported. I wanted some leverage in case she cheated me. I walked away with your baba. I took the fresh start. But I walked away without my son."

Her voice cracked as she looked out the window. "You do not need to judge me. I judge myself every day for leaving him behind. I regret my decision. In my dreams and in every waking moment since. So I always found reasons to be nearby."

The traffic lurched forward and then stopped.

I touched my lip. "Leave *him* behind? You mean me, right?"

Mama took another drag of her cigarette before answering. "A year later, she had surgery done on my baby to fix the lip as best as they could. But she never stopped believing she was given damaged goods. It was such backward thinking. In her eyes, I was the cheat. But it was your uncle, desperate for a son, who insisted on keeping him."

Him, again. I was confused. "She was always kind to me."

"You are the son she wishes she had—smart, respectful, special ... not that child who was born." My brain cramped as this wasn't making sense, causing me to almost ram a bus.

"Your auntie was too stung with jealousy over her husband's betrayal to see that Leo is also all those things and much more." Mama whispered, "Leo is my first-born, your big brother."

"Leo?"

"Hai lo." She cracked a youthful, innocent smile I'd not seen before. Finally, my brain started to clear. Leo's uneven moustache ...

I was putting the pieces together. "It was after Leo's baba died that you started going to the Association regularly. You were going to see Leo." It was so weird saying that. *Leo's my half bro?* "That's way too far out. What kind of a deal is that? What are you trying to tell me?"

"Hai lo," she said again. "Your uncle had forbidden my presence. When he died, your aunt welcomed my presence so she could torment me with her mean-spiritedness toward Leo. Her bad marriage and barrenness may not have been her fault, but they weren't my fault, either. As if giving up my son wasn't enough. Perhaps her play is to impress her triad friends with the special-delivery business you created. I can see her turning Leo into a triad member and her trying to do the same to you. It would destroy me. Perhaps that is also her plan."

"Why did you borrow so much money, and fall behind on payments?"

She twisted her lip. "I sent money home. We all do this. Business was slow, and your baba would have lost his mind had he discovered I took out a loan from the Association. In this case, my mother fell ill. She hasn't been able to work. I could not let her and everyone else go hungry and become homeless. The Association used to lend with low interest and lots of time for repayment in times like these. But now she has taken over the Association and has changed the terms of their loans. She has been cultivating relationships with the triads. It pains me that Leo and now you are being drawn in."

I parked in front of the Association. Buddha Boy, Stanley, and another triad thug emerged from under the hood of a car and gave us the hairy eyeball. Once they recognized Mama, they smiled and nodded respectfully, then returned to their business.

I stayed in the driver's seat. "Maybe we should do this another time. Or I could work for her for one year, and we'll all be free of her."

"We cannot turn back," Mama said. "You'd still have to chop off one of Barry's fingers. Can you do that?"

I shuddered.

"I did not think so. She will never let you go."

"Does Leo know any of this?"

She shook her head. "I doubt your aunt would tell him about her husband bedding me."

There it was again, the Association's front door, so soon after my butt had gotten whupped. I hesitated. Watching my mother go down with me would be worse, way worse.

Chapter 48

The Challenge

THE ASSOCIATION'S SHARP smells of Tiger Balm and old clothes felt familiar and comforting—an odd feeling, given the circumstances. The uncles seemed to sense something. All joking, gossiping, cursing, and snoring ceased when we walked in. One player at a table stopped midmotion. Others around the table followed suit. The uncles' eyes were on the mahjong board Mama was carrying. They tracked Mama's purposeful strides up the stairs.

"Good luck," Uncle Kwong shouted. The others chimed in after him: *Good luck! Good luck!*

"For the children," Uncle Kwong said. That sounded cheesy and embarrassed me at first. But I sensed children meant not only me but theirs—wherever they were.

Mama nodded to them but never broke stride.

Leo intercepted us and half bowed to Mama. He joked and said I could've taken the rest of the day off before the actual work with him began tomorrow.

I studied his face, his uneven moustache. Always that carousel of bowling shirts. This time his shirt was nameless. Mama smiled and said I was not there to work today or ever. We were there to play his mother.

Leo glanced at me and then shrugged before going to get her.

We heard her before we saw her: the sound of her plastic slippers shuffling along the cracked floor.

"Tell me, does the family that loses together stay together?" Auntie said, chuckling.

"Johnny is not for you to take." Mama rolled up her sleeves.

"That is not for you to decide." Auntie led us into the gaming room. "I'm sure Mr. Ho and Char Lai would like an opportunity to win back what they lost."

"I have more favourable terms for you." Mama outlined the challenge and the stakes.

Auntie's eyes widened eagerly. "You are willing to wager yourself for three years?"

"Hai lo. Come, let's play. You and I, no one else. A single rack, four games, six-point-minimum winning hand, three for going out. Otherwise, scoring remains the same. It'll be like when you first showed me how to play." Mama made it sound like this would be fun.

Auntie hesitated at these terms. "How wonderfully nostalgic. You remember I taught you to play. But you learned to lose on your own. I can be a romantic as well. This is why we will play a traditional four-player game."

"No." Mama presented a new case of tiles still in their shiny, clear plastic wrap. "This is so there will be no misunderstanding about which of us is the stronger player."

"There never has been. I beat you regularly."

I was about to say she did this by cheating, but Mama gently squeezed my arm. "Let us look at this as a new game, a fresh start for us. A new beginning."

"How do I know you won't simply leave?"

"You know why I return. I always have." Mama quickly glanced at Leo before staring Auntie down. "I have always honoured any agreement between us. Once I beat you, you leave me, my Johnny, and the restaurant alone. Dissolve my loan. You will honour this, because you wouldn't want other gamblers to believe you acted dishonourably."

"And Barry," I said.

Auntie laughed. "Ah, the Golden Boy. He doesn't matter. You won't win, regardless of what we play. Fine, let's play."

Chapter 49

Big Three Dragons

LEO UNWRAPPED MAMA's new case of tiles and placed them on the table. Her eyes lingered on him. I'd never noticed before.

I stood against the wall, several feet behind her, as she and Auntie wordlessly shuffled the tiles, which sounded like ice cubes clinking together. They stacked them into walls. A roll of the dice determined that Auntie would start the game. They each drew thirteen tiles, with Auntie drawing a fourteenth. Her discard would start the game.

Like always, Auntie neither looked at nor organized her tiles. Instead, her thumb rubbed the engravings, and she left them face down. It was the psych-out starting move we expected. I wanted to believe Mama had this. But before I knew it, Auntie was feasting on Mama's discards, scoring runs and pungs regularly, whereas Mama was standing still. Auntie quickly took the first game with runs across different suits, then the second game with three of a kind—pungs. Beginner-level hands, not big points, but she was building a winning streak, and Mama had fallen behind.

They took a break. Mama stood, stretched like she'd been napping, and lit a cigarette.

"What are you doing? Are you trying to lose?" I whispered.

"You must be good to be lucky, and she's been lucky. So far."

Auntie started shuffling the tiles, signalling Mama to return to what I feared would be a rout.

"Remember when we first played together, not long after I arrived?" Mama asked Auntie. "Uncle was always working, so there was only you and me. That is, until he started spending more time with me. You know what I am saying."

Auntie froze momentarily.

"You were a master at revealing the game within the game," Mama said. "How to use your head and not just the tiles. Remember?"

Auntie scrunched her nose, as though the memory were fermented shrimp paste left uncovered overnight, then continued shuffling the tiles.

"You were a good teacher—strict but patient. I remember you saying you wanted to be a teacher, but Uncle said that was a silly idea, that your accent was too strong and you'd never get hired. Besides, Uncle wanted you to run the laundry."

Auntie slapped down a few tiles that had turned over. "That was a long time ago. Now, who cares? Let's play. Stop delaying."

"It was long ago. But I still remember." She discarded a 6 Bamboo. Auntie snatched it and turned it into a three of a kind before dumping a North Wind, which was useless for Mama. I didn't like the look of that.

Instead, Mama picked another tile from the wall and immediately threw it away. Again, Auntie stole it, revealing a run of 5-6-7 Bamboos. Her blank face broke into a grin. I guess she couldn't help it. She was likely waiting for a final tile to win. Was Mama going to cough up something valuable only for Auntie to snatch it? I had to turn away.

Leo's eyes darted back and forth. I wondered what he'd be like to work with. Would he be the evil big brother I'd never had or just someone cool to hang with?

Mama's next two pickups went straight into the discard pile. I held my breath, expecting Auntie to turn them into points. She was hammering Mama. But Auntie passed. Still, in three hands, Mama had yet to reveal any combos. Was she flaming out that badly or purposely playing concealed hands? I saw what Auntie was playing for. For sure, Mama could see it, too.

Mama stole a 9 Character, scoring a pung. But she dropped a 5 Bamboo, which Auntie immediately used to flip, arranging her winning sets to reveal a semi-pure hand of bamboo and honour tiles, just as I'd figured. How had Mama not seen that coming? Auntie had amassed a considerable lead with one game left.

Arghhh, I wanted to scream at Mama. She took a breath but didn't show any panic. What was she thinking? I'd expected her to put up more of a fight. Now, I was realizing I was condemned. Auntie and the triads would never release me. The unmistakable heaviness of fried food and weed would permanently settle into my clothes, skin, and hair. I would be the egg roll man, the Chinese food guy with the special herb. People would say, "I can't remember his name, let's just call him

Bruce." Suddenly, I heard every slur, every slight, every prejudiced remark and dismissive look I'd ever gotten while delivering Chinese food. My clenched fists dug into my pockets.

I couldn't watch, so I squeezed my eyes shut. "Mama, take a break." I wanted to tap her shoulder but remembered how touching someone at the table was considered bad luck. She didn't need any more of that. Thankfully, she got the hint and stood.

I had a cup of tea ready for her. "You can do it, Mama." I doubt I sounded very encouraging as she sipped away.

Auntie soon waved Mama back. "Enough. And still, the student cannot defeat me. You should have paid better attention during those lessons."

It was like a nightmare unfolding. With so much on the line, Mama just shrugged again. I'd seen her more upset about the rice boiling over. I couldn't understand her.

"Maybe, but remember you paraded me around Chinatown like I was your daughter? That was the most I ever saw you smile."

Auntie winced. She was old now. I'd bet it'd been a while since anybody brought that up with her.

"You would've liked a daughter, one of your own," Mama said. "You would've protected her with a fierceness."

Auntie hesitated as the colour drained from her face. "Stop talking about things that no longer matter."

Mama hadn't won any games, but she seemed to have landed a blow. Was this her play?

Mama shuffled for one last game. After three straight losses, she hadn't wavered. Instead, she began to hum with an unmistakable lilt in her voice. The song was familiar. It took me a moment, but I'd heard her sing it a few weeks back as we formed egg rolls together. It was the ballad, "A Young Girl's Dream."

Her hands moved fluidly over the crashing tiles. Bamboo, bone, and ivory flowed together like water. Mama's humming and the reverberation of the tiles were like a jagged ensemble of instruments—our opera.

Auntie shifted uncomfortably and tried to ignore Mama's joy. Leo also noticed and stifled a smile. My feet tapped along in synch with Mama's humming.

"Stop!" Auntie shrieked. "This is not a party. No wonder you are losing. Where is your focus? Can you not take this seriously?"

Auntie's words bounced off Mama, who continued to shuffle before building the wall. "I am taking this seriously. You're winning. Why aren't you singing and dancing?"

"Do you not understand what is at stake? Your son—"

"They will always be my *sons*."

Auntie banged the table with her fist, shaking the room.

Leo's face creased.

"Why didn't you get mad when your husband strayed?" Mama asked. "Why did you not bang the table then?"

Ouch! It was unbelievable that Mama would say this in front of us. In this war of words, she'd just pulled out a cleaver.

Auntie fumed. "You have no idea what living with your uncle and holding everything together was like."

Mama nodded. "Maybe not."

"Play, no more talking."

"You're right. I don't know what it was like for you. But what do you think happened while you were home and Uncle and I were left managing the laundry?"

Auntie froze. Leo froze.

"Back then," Mama said, "we did as we were told, including keeping quiet. Win or lose, those days are over."

Auntie slammed several tiles as her nostrils flared. She had just about lost it.

Leo glanced around the room, unable to land on something familiar.

They formed their racks, but Auntie flipped hers over this time and grouped them like the other mortals.

Auntie opened the door by discarding a Red Dragon, which Mama quickly converted into a pung of three Red Dragons. Then Auntie hesitated, which I had never seen her do before. She didn't take Mama's discard but held onto her draw from the wall.

They rotated useless pickups before Auntie picked up Mama's discard, revealing 4, 5, and 6 Bamboos. Auntie's face slackened as some of her old self returned. She only had to go out to win, whereas Mama had to score one of the biggest hands possible. That'd be like pulling your goalie and scoring three goals to win.

Auntie picked up Mama's next discard and scored another run. She had seven tiles remaining. Who knew if she was already waiting to win on a final combo. Was she taunting Mama?

I leaned over and saw Mama with pairs of green and white dragons—and the rest of the circle tiles already composed into a three-of-a-kind pair. I craned my neck and understood what Mama was playing for: the big three dragons. I'd only ever heard rumours of hands like that. She picked up a Green Dragon, completing a three of a kind of the second dragon. She discarded a 5 Character, which Auntie seized, revealing a 4-5-6 run. Auntie had only four tiles left. She probably had a pair and was waiting on one final tile to complete a last run to seal her and Mama's fate.

My heart thundered as the play continued. Mama discarded a nine. Auntie bit her lip and looked at Mama. Her big lead would be meaningless if Mama pulled off a big hand. Mama needed a final White Dragon to complete the big three dragons. She could win by converting her pair of circles into a three of a kind, but it wouldn't make for a big enough hand to win it all.

Auntie tried a psych-out look on Mama as if to say it was over. But Mama ignored her and drew from the wall. Without looking at the tile, she carefully massaged the engraving, then placed the tile down, face up, revealing a White Dragon.

"Sik wu," she whispered before exposing her hand. Her eyes locked onto Auntie, who gasped as she studied Mama's tiles. The big three dragons, won by jee moh—self-drawing—absolutely unheard of.

I just about jumped in the air. Mama's and Auntie's eyes remained locked on one another. No one blinked. Finally, Auntie turned to Leo. I thought she would tell him to get Barry and release him to us. Instead, she instructed him to show me around and said I would be with them for a long while.

"No. I won! Fair and square. We had a deal." Mama pounded the table, losing her cool for a second.

"Was it fair? How do I know these tiles aren't marked? No one beats me unless they've cheated."

I was about to accuse her of cheating when Mama's arm shot out to hold me back. "You know a thing or two about cheating. My Johnny watched you and Mr. Ho. I might have known, but I was too naïve and looked the other way. I wanted to believe you were good enough on your own."

"I am."

"More importantly, I believed you were good inside. I once believed that about you. Then Uncle hardened you. But we no longer have to bite our tongues and swallow our humiliation as others run our lives. We don't have to be like that anymore."

Auntie blinked.

"We need to move on. Live your life."

"Hmmph." Auntie waved her off. "What nonsense. You don't get to leave me again." Auntie's nostrils flared. "Leo, show Johnny around his new job. They cheated, and for that, he is mine. They both are."

"Johnny, go get Barry," Mama commanded.

Leo stepped from behind Auntie and in front of me. He lifted his arm. I winced, expecting him to start pounding me. Instead, he opened the door and ushered us out.

"Mother, if people think we cheat on family and won't accept a loss, business will suffer." Leo looked at Auntie, who stood and stared him down. Leo held his ground.

"Leo's right," I said. "I will run my mouth. I'll make it my business to warn everybody. No one will play with you again." I edged closer, taking in her stare. "And we're not leaving without Barry."

"No," Auntie shouted. "The Golden Boy is ours."

"Gaa je, we have fought for too long. Yet we have always honoured our agreements, all of them."

That was the only time I'd ever heard Mama call Auntie "big sister."

Auntie lowered herself onto her chair and scrambled the tiles, half throwing them across the table.

"It was wrong of me to say 'my' sons. You raised Leo as well as any mother could. And you were an aunt to Johnny and me. Let this go."

Leo's eyes darted between Mama and Auntie. His mouth parted as if he wanted to ask a question but couldn't get it out.

Mama left the table, leaving Auntie to hide behind her visor.

"Hey, Leo . . ." I was about to ask him to follow us. I wanted to tell him everything I'd just discovered, but I stopped. That was Mama and Auntie's story to tell. Instead, I asked if he wanted to see *Star Wars* with me. It's really good, and I wanted to watch it again. I wanted his company.

He shrugged. "Why not?"

Mama gave him a smile that was as warm as any hug. She patted my hand like I was still a boy. I should have been embarrassed and kept my hand to myself. Instead, I let her show me the way out even though we'd been here many times.

The uncles looked at Mama and me as we descended the stairs. Uncle Kwong banged his teacup against the table, grinning with approval. The other uncles followed suit.

"My mama, the tiger tamer," I said to the uncles, who chuckled.

She could've basked in the moment with a triumphant cheer and shaken all their hands. Instead, she made do with a simple smile. She was more concerned with getting Barry to the hospital.

Chapter 50

Bye, Bye, Barry

MAMA AND I sat in the Mount Sinai emergency waiting room while Barry was being treated. She surprised me by asking how Angie was.

I wanted to say she was dead to me, a user, a phony, and nothing special. But Mama would've seen through that. I leaned my shoulder against hers. I missed Angie. Even though she was nearby in school every day, and in my head, I still missed her. That made it more complicated.

"It's like you said. She'll make the choices she must make. I shouldn't be angry that she's able to do it. I don't know how she's doing. But she's special." I'll continue fantasizing about her, but deep down, I know our orbits don't align.

The doctor examining Barry came out to ask what had happened. We said he'd fallen off a motorcycle several days ago but had been too proud to come in. She raised an eyebrow, clearly not believing us, but she treated him anyway. Barry had a fractured rib, a broken nose, a couple of missing teeth, and severe bruising in several places. Hours later, Barry insisted on going home to get some things. He said he could find somewhere safe to hang out for a while. Mama said she didn't think Auntie would send anybody after him.

"I'm not taking any chances," he whispered. He didn't sound scared or even angry, just exhausted. "You Chinamen play rough. I can't count on her not coming after me."

Mama made it look like she'd heard nothing, but my fists balled and dug into my pockets. For a second, I wished they had cut Barry's tongue out, but then I just said, "That's a shitty thing to say, Barry, considering I just saved your life."

"I'd have done the same for you."

That was true, although I wouldn't have gotten him into such a mess in the first place. It wasn't his fault Mama owed money, and I'd agreed to go in on the drug-dealing with him, but had I known he'd recklessly stolen from the wrong people—no way. He was lucky he hadn't lost any fingers—or worse. I wanted to tell him to piss off. But he'd already gotten the crap beaten out of him.

Mom cabbed it home while I took Barry back to his place. I helped him stuff a duffle bag.

He'd popped back into our lives out of the blue. We'd had some fun. I used to think I could never repay what I owed him as a kid. To add to that debt, he hadn't weaseled his way out with Auntie by trying to blame the theft on me. Does that mean I owe him a lifetime of feeling guilty, though? Look where that got Mama. But I'd saved his ass. We were even.

He sagged beneath his bag.

I emptied my wallet and handed him what I had. There wasn't much, but it would have to do.

"Let's go to the Zanzibar. I need to get hammered," he said.

"No."

"Then the Brunswick House. The draft is cheaper."

"No, Barry. I think we should take a break."

"Take a break? What are we, breaking up?" He tried to laugh, but it hurt him too much.

"Yeah, you're too much for me. I need to get my life together, not light it on fire. And I can't take your heat and your humour anymore."

We studied one another until it became awkwardly quiet.

He shook his head like I was being an asshole, like I'd let him down the way everyone eventually did.

"I hope you find your mother," I said.

He shook his head. "I don't think it'll make any difference."

I did feel shitty. He wasn't the bad guy here. Yet it felt like I'd done something overdue. All I had to do was not swallow his shit anymore.

I offered a handshake, which he ignored and left. I suppose he'd had many goodbyes already and maybe didn't have another in him. He would survive.

The next day, Mama and I spoke with Mr. Miller. We told him what he needed to know. She explained that my drug days were over and that they'd be keeping a closer eye on me. He was sympathetic and promised he wouldn't inform anyone of my short-lived weed-delivery service. But he had a condition, a pretty big one.

Chapter 51

A Farewell to Kings

MAMA AND BABA kept the restaurant running. When Mama returned home to Hong Kong for a month to visit her mother, we had to hire extra staff.

Jane took over the daily sandwich board and replaced Bruce's sayings with *Star Trek* quotes, such as:

> *Beam me up some Chinese food, Scotty.*

On my last day in Toronto, I got up early to finish packing for college. I was in the middle of it when Jane entered my room and handed me a present wrapped in tissue paper. "I got it at Sam the Record Man."

I just about shit myself.

"Relax, I paid for it."

I unwrapped a T-shirt and merch from Rush's latest album, *A Farewell to Kings*, which I'd been playing on the turntable. It fit perfectly. I told her I felt bad—I hadn't gotten her anything.

A car pulled up. Someone knocked on the door below, quickly followed by footsteps up the stairs. Andrew and Baahir entered my bedroom. They were also wearing Rush T-shirts. It all felt pretty groovy, and we sang along to the title track.

"You sure you don't want to come?" I asked Jane.

"To squeeze into that Pinto to a Rush concert in Rochester? And then drive five more hours to Hartford to see a hockey game? I'd rather poke my eyes out. But it's nice to be asked, thanks." She smiled. "Hang on a second."

She pulled out Baba's Kodak and commanded us to say "Rush rats!" as she took our picture.

Just as we finished loading up, Mama intercepted us. "Your baba is busy. He couldn't be here."

Baba was supposed to help load the car and see me off, but he'd been treating me like I was radioactive. Was he mad at me? Had I done something wrong? Baba had said very little to me after I accepted the scholarship. He'd warned me that writing wouldn't put food on the table, that I'd be wasting time and money. Outside of those moments, I was all but invisible to him.

I promised myself that, if I ever became a father, I would be a different kind of baba. I would help my kids reach their potential and encourage them to approach challenges, confront fears, and seize every opportunity that comes their way—unless it's to work in a Chinese restaurant. I'd disown them if they did that, unless cooking was their passion.

"He's at the bank," Mama said. "It just came up. It did. He wanted to be here."

"Really?" I wanted to slam the door on my way out. "His son goes off to college, and he goes AWOL?"

She deflected my anger with her maternal reflexes. "Drive carefully, lock your doors, and don't talk to strangers." Like I was still a child. "You have the tickets?"

I nodded and patted the pocket in my denim jacket, which held three tickets for a Hartford Whalers game the following night. The ones Mama had surprised me with.

"Dave Keon will be there," she said.

I was surprised she even knows who my childhood hero is. I've always created someone to look out for me, from Dave Keon to Bruce Lee, but I'd never realized that an opera-loving Chinglish speaker I get to call Mama has been my force field all along.

As Mama loaded the car with snacks, I wondered if I would return, if my parents could keep the restaurant going—or even stay together. They continue to play by the rules: they keep quiet, they work hard, and they never hurt anybody. They had bet everything on the future—Jane and me.

Some people, like Auntie, don't play by the rules until they get caught. After Mama beat her, she kept playing the game. She might have gotten away with her triad dealings. But a new police liaison was hired, who visited the Association and made it clear he worked for the police and no one else, meaning he wasn't being paid off and couldn't be intimidated. With Uncle Kwong and the other uncles looking on, the liaison warned that police raids would follow. They had intel. The Association might have to shut down.

Uncle Kwong and I had egg custard tarts at Yung Sing's one day. He told me about Auntie threatening to kick them all out. She said she wasn't running a charity anymore. Uncle Kwong and the other uncles exchanged glances. Their era was going out like the last inches of a burning joss stick. Where would they go? They had one final play. With Uncle Kwong leading the way, the uncles gathered their arthritic joints, weak vision, and deaf ears and stood up to Auntie.

"We lose each other if we lose the Association. Nothing could be worse. Soon enough, we will each be carried out of this life forever. But you must drag us out if you want us to leave."

Auntie laughed at them. But Uncle Kwong and his stern determination were as fierce as the battle cry of any muscled-up general. Neither Leo nor any goons would forcibly remove them. Auntie backed down and returned the management of the Association to the uncles. It was an overdue victory for them. I realized that the loyalty and unspeakable loneliness that marked the uncles' lives didn't mean they'd wasted their lives but that they'd paid their lives forward. They expect me to make good on that.

With few debts worth chasing and all the high-stakes games banished, the triads moved on. It probably cost Auntie some serious coin to get the triads to allow her to walk away.

Having lost face, Auntie went to Hong Kong.

Leo and I occasionally have beers. He sees my mama—our mama, from time to time. Mama insists on him still calling her "Auntie." It's an olive branch to his mother.

Leo and I still haven't talked much about our family. We haven't called each other "brother," although we float a few "bros" like all guys do. We're cool keeping things as is. It's safe to stick to beers and hockey. One day, while we were sitting at Grossman's Tavern, he said he'd always wanted to see Hong Kong and that he was finally going. But he wasn't very convincing. Auntie was there, and I was sure she'd pulled him back into her orbit.

Mama and Auntie haven't spoken since that mahjong game. The vast mist remains.

Chapter 52

Be Like Water

ATTENDING WESTERN CONNECTICUT State was Mr. Miller's condition for not going to the police. I wandered around campus before the first day of classes, thinking about how luck brought me here.

Like Mama, Bruce never believed in pure luck.

He said we must create our luck. After all, life is made of time (something Uncle Kwong also said), and you can't waste time waiting. So he took charge, went away, and created his destiny. It's similar for me. Instead of a wobbly life, I'll make mine a straight path. Inevitably, it will lead back to my family, whether they need rescuing or not.

I watched a father help his son unload his things outside of the college residency. It saddens me that Baba wouldn't do that for me. Truthfully, Baba checked out on me long ago. I hate how Baba not being around reminds me of Bruce Lee's death. I'm bad at talking about it, so I don't. I mean, we Chinese suck at talking. It's a special order we don't do. Avoidance and silence are always on the menu, though.

At times, I'm conflicted about Bruce's legacy. No disrespect, I loved the movies, but his films didn't show enough of him being the fighter who didn't fight: the thinker, the philosopher. I know he tried working that in, but the studios just wanted action, and so did the people buying tickets.

He always talked about fulfilling your potential and having faith in yourself. For him, actions spoke louder than words. Knowing was not enough. He believed in doing. He didn't walk the talk. He sprinted it. Maybe he just needed to jog occasionally. Ultimately, that was his big mistake.

A stream of Bruce fights run through my head. Bruce kicking, punching, biting, and doing whatever it takes. He lost twenty pounds while making *Enter the Dragon* and almost died two months before his final collapse. Instead of heeding the red light, he cranked up the energy even more, sending his mind and body into warp speed. Even for someone as energetic and determined as Bruce Lee, it couldn't last.

Even philosopher kings and martial arts gods fall.

Because of Bruce, we are seen. He changed martial arts. Those Taoist sayings of his that sound like fortune cookies are cool now, and they do have nuggets of wisdom. Now, more Chinese dare to stand up to the gwai lo. We have the courage to endure and forge our path. He helped show us that. Some days it feels like we traded sideways, giving up the meek Chinaman role for the butt-kicking martial artist. We're neither of those. What are we, then?

At the very least, I can be proud of who I am, which would make Bruce very happy.

So, if Bruce could fall and be loved, maybe someday I can let my shit about Auntie and Baba go.

Even dead, Bruce gave me the strength to work things through.

In my first days living away from home, I kept wandering around campus, deep in thought, lonely, and despite feeling proud of myself, I also worried I would fail. Then Bruce suddenly appeared. Months had passed since I last saw him. For once, he wasn't in workout mode. He was calm, and we stood eye to eye for the first time. Bruce was taller than me, but maybe he was slouching from weariness. Or maybe I'd learned to stand straighter.

He smiled. "Hey, man. Aiming low and doing nothing is a crime. You may be afraid, but don't fear failure. You no longer need me."

He'd never called me "man" before.

"I have often heard you say that you are not me. But Johnny, you are yourself. I am proud of you. You should be too."

He pulled out two nunchucks, placed them on the ground, and bowed to me. I wanted to tell him I had seen a picture of his kids the other day. They'd grown and looked great.

Instead, I had a final question. "If you could do it all over again, would you do anything differently?"

"Would you? If we did, then we wouldn't be who we are." He turned away and slowly began to fade.

I stepped up to reach for him but was almost cut off by a student walking by, a real beefcake. The beefcake glared at me, got in my face, and told me to watch my step. Then he said that I looked familiar, that he'd seen me somewhere.

My body tensed. I was waiting for the insult and was ready to tell him off. My instinct was to look for Bruce. I took a deep breath and followed his flow:

Empty your mind, be formless—shapeless, like water. If you put water into a cup, it becomes the cup. You put water into a bottle, and it becomes the bottle. You put it in a teapot. It becomes the teapot. Now, water can flow, or it can crash. Be water, my friend.

Bruce disappeared for the last time. I decided I could be water.

"You're thinking of my bro, Bruce," I told the beef-cake. "He's gone for good. But I'm Johnny, Johnny Wong." I extended my hand and smiled. "Pleased to meet you."

Author's Note

Johnny Delivers is a work of fiction, although I wanted to integrate personal and historical elements from 1977. As the son of Chinese immigrants, I was born and raised in downtown Toronto. My father worked as a chef at Lichee Garden, and I had many relatives who ran Chinese restaurants. I worshipped Bruce Lee and watched his films at the Pagoda Theatre. I lived on Henry Street and attended Central Technical School, skipping classes to play pinball and smoke at Manny's and Nick's.

The Chinese head tax passed by the Canadian government, the Chinese Exclusion Act, the tongs, also known as associations, and the arrival of the triads in the 1970s are all matters of historical record. My grandfather Ng Men Chem paid the head tax in 1911.

What is less known are the other draconian measures placed upon the Chinese in Canada. Other immigrant groups were not immune to racism, but none experienced the systemic brutality inflicted upon the Chinese, who were racially profiled, registered, numbered, interrogated, and tracked. The threat of a severe fine, imprisonment, and deportation was never far, even for those born in Canada. Because of such measures and the history of exclusion, many Chinese could only enter the country through forged documents, leading to the term *paper sons* and *daughters*. Many paper children (such as my mother and an uncle) kept this secret, leaving many with little connection to any family history.

For more information, visit the Chinese Canadian Museum and the Chinatown Storytelling Centre in Vancouver, British Columbia.

Acknowledgements

Thank you, readers, for taking *Johnny Delivers* for a ride. I also want to thank the writing community and all the people who generously gave their time and support to my writing, especially:

Trish Lucy, my beloved, for everything.

Margo LaPierre, my editor extraordinaire, for the joy of working in synchronicity, seeing beyond words, and delivering *Johnny* home.

Guernica Editions (Michael Mirolla, Anna van Valkenburg, Crystal Fletcher, Connie Guzzo-McParland) for providing a publishing family unafraid of taking risks.

June Chow for her expertise on mahjong, Cantonese, and Chinese Canadian history and her patience as an authenticity reader.

Arlene Chan for her deep knowledge of Chinese Canadian history and Chinese associations.

Howard Dock for beta reading and for his knowledge about paper sons and family-owned Chinese restaurants.

Joe LaFortune for his detailed beta reading, his expertise of all things seventies, Rush, and for being my inside man at Zanzibar.

Doreen Arnoni for her humour, always stepping up and editing the rough stuff.

Roger Seto for sharing his delivery stories and helping with Chinese restaurants, tongs, and triads.

Cedar Faucette, Karel Nelson, and Aarthi Cloutier for being my young beta readers.

Marc Brown for his knowledge and awareness of dried herbs and how it was moved.

My wonderful critiquing group—Chris Crowder, Amy Tector, and Alette Willis—for their keen analysis of the first draft.

Allan Cho and Todd Wong of the Asian Canadian Writers' Workshop Society (ACWW) for their friendship and commitment to promoting Asian writers.

Mahj Life, a.k.a. Michele Frizzell, for her expertise on mahjong.

Jeffrey Wong, Aynsley Wong, and the Wongs' Benevolent Association of Canada.

Branka Milin-Campbell, for bravely sharing her memories of Central Technical School.

Hollay Ghadery for epitomizing literary friendship and citizenship.

Eddy Ng for being a bro.

The Central Technical School Alumni Facebook group.

My Orde Street Public School and Lord Lansdowne Senior Public School childhood friends.

Dave Keon for still being a hero and a gentleman.

Bruce Lee for inspiring generations.

The Chinese Canadian Museum and the Chinatown Storytelling Centre for keeping our stories alive.

Three remarkable artist residencies: the Historic Joy Kogawa House, Eastern Frontier Educational Foundation, and La Napoule Art Foundation for providing me with wonderful experiences that foster creative energy and lifelong memories.

The Canada Council for the Arts and the BC Arts Council for their generous support of this project.

About the Author

WAYNE NG was born in downtown Toronto to Chinese immigrants who fed him a steady diet of bitter melon and kung fu movies. Ng is a social worker who lives to write, travel, eat, and play, preferably all at the same time. He is an award-winning author and traveller who continues to push his boundaries from the Arctic to the Antarctic. He lives in Ottawa with his wife and goldfish. Ng is also the author of *The Family Code*, shortlisted for the Guernica Prize; *Letters From Johnny*, winner of the Crime Writers of Canada Award for Best Crime Novella and a finalist for the Ottawa Book Award; and *Finding the Way: A Novel of Lao Tzu.*

Connect with Ng on social media and at:
waynengwrites.com

Printed by Imprimerie Gauvin
Gatineau, Québec